THE HOUNDING

THE HOUNDING

XENOBE PURVIS

HENRY HOLT AND COMPANY
NEW YORK

Henry Holt and Company
Publishers since 1866
120 Broadway
New York, New York 10271
www.henryholt.com

Henry Holt® and Ⓗ® are registered trademarks of
Macmillan Publishing Group, LLC.

Distributed in Canada by Raincoast Book Distribution Limited

Library of Congress Cataloging-in-Publication Data is available.

ISBN 9781250366382

Our books may be purchased in bulk for promotional, educational, or business use. Please contact your local bookseller or the Macmillan Corporate and Premium Sales Department at (800) 221-7945, extension 5442, or by e-mail at MacmillanSpecialMarkets@macmillan.com.

First U.S. Edition 2025

Designed by Kelly S. Too

Printed in the United States of America

1 3 5 7 9 10 8 6 4 2

For my parents

Last summer a great rumour spread to us that some young girls . . . in the Oxfordshire countryside had been seized with frequent barking in the manner of dogs.

—Dr. John Friend, "Letter to the Editor, concerning a Tale of Rare Convulsions," *Philosophical Transactions of the Royal Society* (1701)

THE HOUNDING

THE GIRLS, THE INFERNAL HEAT, A FRESH-DEAD BODY. Marching up the river path, the villagers—adorned with gaudy ribbons, some carrying stones—saw exactly what had taken place. The girls had found their quarry at last; the bite mark on the man's fist, the spreading blood, spoke of an unholy struggle.

Anne, the eldest sister, stood ahead of the others, and the advancing rabble watched her warily. Some said she had been the first to change, barking in the barren lane by their home. No, others insisted, it started with the littlest, then leapt through the rest like a contagion: Mary first, timid Grace went next, then Hester the tomboy, pretty Elizabeth, and lastly puzzling, peculiar Anne.

The idea of it was enough to turn anyone on their heel, but the villagers told themselves they had nothing to fear. There were too many of them, a vengeful mob; no girl could withstand them, not even wicked ones such as these—black dresses masking bushy tails, pretty mouths filled with pointed yellow teeth. How good it felt, how safe and enfolding, walking shoulder to shoulder towards a shared enemy. The cracked ground trembled beneath their feet.

They chanted the sisters' names as they approached. *Anne, Elizabeth, Hester, Grace, Mary*—as though to remind them that they were merely girls. Not dogs nor demons: undistinguished girls. Dirt lifted underfoot, powdering their clothes, their wedding best. They were angry. Perhaps not only about the sisters or the murdered man's fate. They were angry about the weather and their failing crops and shallow wells, alongside all sorts of ordinary things, like the fact that their wives no longer loved them or that they would someday die.

Anne, Elizabeth, Hester, Grace, Mary. Ribbons danced in the bright summer sun. The river, weakened by weeks of scorching heat, traversed a bed of husks and bones. The villagers drew near to the body. Unspeaking, the sisters watched them come.

ONE

Pete Darling had seen many things waiting for him across the water. Sometimes he saw faces familiar to him from the village—men idling alone, maidservants in huddled pairs. The vicar, grimacing, the hem of his cassock pulled up to his calves so it didn't meet with any mud. Occasionally Pete found animals. An ox and cart heaped high with hay. A boy with a squealing piglet beneath each armpit. A single hen. (It amused him to think she had business on the other side; he ferried her across without charging a fare.)

Once, after a few too many pints, he thought he saw in the purple dusk an angel waiting for him at the water's edge. The angel seemed to him to be made of soft light, like dancing flames. Awed, Pete ferried the angel across the dark water, but when they reached the far bank he looked away for a moment and turned back to discover that his punt was empty. This didn't diminish the significance of the visitation for Pete. He believed he was in some way special, in some way chosen. He had borne an angel across the River Thames; sacred feet, burning and bright, had touched the splintering wood of his old ferry.

Nothing much surprised him as he surveyed the bank from

his seat in the alehouse window. He had learned this unflusteredness from his father, a ferryman before him, who looked up one day to find a row of soldiers standing on the river's edge. Soldiers were no strange thing in the village then, it being the civil war and the fight for England's king raging in fields all over Oxfordshire, but these ones seemed to Pete's father like something from a dream. Sprigs of willow were fixed to their caps and wound like crowns around their heads. Weeds grew from their cuffs and pockets, encircling their waists. Flowers sprang from their buttonholes. On the river, he had asked them why they were bedecked in leaves and trailing branches. To tell them apart from the other side, one soldier said, spitting; their coats were the same colour. Growing up, Pete often heard about these green soldiers and accepted the lesson they delivered: that the riverbank might present him with any number of peculiarities, all of which it was his duty to endure.

Whatever awaited him there, his response was the same. He would finish his drink, push himself up from his stool, and trudge unhurriedly down the dirt path to the rushes where his punt was tied. He had been doing this job since he was a boy, just tall enough to wield the pole. He would be doing this job for a long time more—or at least while bridges stayed away from this bend in the river.

That day, however, glancing at the far bank, he felt uneasy. Five girls were waiting there, old Joseph Mansfield's granddaughters. At first, through mottled glass, the girls looked odd to him, changed somehow: pale faces lined up in a row, like petals roughly shaken from a rosebush. Wild, inhuman—not girls at all. Five drifts of snow. Five fallen moons.

When they required him, people usually gestured from across the river, but the girls did nothing. They stood completely still.

He couldn't see whether they spoke to each other or smiled. He felt a pricking at the back of his neck as he drained his drink and stood up to go.

He pressed the pole into the bed of the river—rock here, not mud as in other places—and began to make his way across. The ferry cut through brown water. Lapwings dipped overhead; the sun was nearing its height. His uneasiness grew greater. It was as if a fever had gripped him; he could feel it in the clamminess of his hands, the way the wood slipped through them.

The ferry knocked against the far bank. He looked up. Not rose petals or snowdrifts—the Mansfield sisters once more. They didn't speak. The eldest handed him some coins, and he felt her fingers hot against his. They stepped onto the punt, one by one, but they were so small and light it barely rocked. The prettiest came last, carrying a large basket of clothes which cast wide ripples around them when she placed it on the wood.

He pushed off gently; the current was weak at this time of year. "Off to Greater Nettlebed, then?"

They were silent. Two of them were kneeling at the edge of the ferry, peering into the water. The pretty one with the basket seemed lost in a daydream. The fourth—fairy-small, fidgety—was frowning at the eldest. The eldest turned and met his eye. "Yes," she said at last.

She said nothing more. Pete found that he was a little afraid of this girl, with her icy gaze and scalding hands. He tried to concentrate on punting, tried not to be distracted by his cargo of dark-haired sisters as they contemplated the water, or fiddled with their dresses, or whispered into one another's ears. He didn't like how agitating he found them. When they disembarked, he reached out and—without quite knowing why—touched the place where the angel had once stood.

A few hours later, the girls returned. This time, he had no uneasy feeling. They were just ordinary girls, nothing to wonder at. Even when the eldest one looked at him directly, encompassing him in her sky-blue stare, he didn't feel discomfited. She was just a girl—he repeated this to himself, blinking, as he felt her attention pass from him to the far bank. She was just a girl. He eyed the back of her head. She had no power over him.

Now it was the fretful, fidgeting one who carried the basket. A shadow had climbed into it: the clothes, brown and blue and parchment yellow on the way over, had become entirely black. "Dyed them, did you?" he said to the girl, sensing that out of all of them—the pretty one, curling a ringlet with a finger over her ear, or the two who had resumed their kneeling watch beside the water, or the eldest, sharing a smiling private joke with her nails—this one was most likely to answer him.

She pulled the basket towards herself and looked at her eldest sister. "Yes," she said.

He pushed the pole into the riverbed, leisurely now. "I was sorry to hear about your grandmother. God rest her soul."

The girl glared at her sister. "Thank you," she said.

"How's old farmer Mansfield? It must be hard without her, with his sight and all."

The girl said nothing, eyes darting to see how far they still had to go.

He tried again. "Will he be getting more help on the farm?"

His tone was friendly. He had, after all, encountered these sisters often before, had seen them through many passing seasons. He had ferried them in summer, his punt swaying beneath the baskets of cherries they sold at market, and in autumn, laden with damsons and golden quinces. He had been their artery to the outside world; everything they required had gone through him. Once, he'd even ferried their cow, Fillpail, steering carefully so as not to startle her. And yet, every time he saw them, they were cold to him.

Now they were ignoring him entirely. He looked at the eldest, at the two at the edge of the ferry, at the pretty one, but they all kept their backs to him. He saw their hands, their delicate wrists. Their dove-white necks. He imagined them floating like feathers on the surface of the river, then sinking slowly, pulled down by their dresses and petticoats. He saw the faces of each of them as though through yards of brown water. Their skin grew green. Blue eyes became black.

Something surged within him then, an unmasterable rage. The sisters seemed not to see him at all, nor to hear him speak. To be disrespected on his own ferry . . . He wouldn't stand for it. This was his dominion. Whatever power the girls had, an indefinable power—stemming from their manyness, their silent disdain—it held no sway here. He stopped punting, letting the pole kiss floating leaves. The ferry began to drift downstream. The girls glanced at each other, and the pretty one gripped the edge of the wood.

It was nothing—a still moment in the middle of the river. The looks the girls exchanged, the way they measured the distance to the bank with their eyes, was fortifying to him. He fed on it like a large meal. He deserved it, after the odd feeling they had given him, after they'd treated his polite enquiries with such contempt. He relished their fear. For a brief moment—no time at all, really—they were within his control.

Still, the girls were silent. The one he had been questioning clutched the basket, her head bowed. The two at the edge scowled at the water. The eldest raised her face to him. He smiled at her. Just a joke, you see. Just resting his arms. The ferry continued to drift.

She frowned at the river. "Come," she said to her sisters. "We'll wade."

The pretty one's eyebrows lifted. She pinched her dress. "Anne, no."

"It's not far. The water's shallow."

This wasn't right. He was the ferryman; he couldn't watch them wade. Not with the little girl. Not with a basket of mourning clothes on their backs. All he wanted was some sign from them that they acknowledged him. That they saw him for what he knew himself to be: a man, a strong man, in the prime of health. A good man, God-fearing, who had been visited by an angel. Not someone to be ignored. He didn't like the way they looked at each other. It was as though they spoke a silent language he couldn't understand; it unsettled him. It made him feel less strong, less good. All he wanted was to be seen.

He was thinking these thoughts, leaning, now, on the pole, so they were no longer floating downstream. Without warning, the eldest girl, Anne, swung her feet to the edge of the ferry and slipped into the water. He stared. She was standing on the rock bed, her cap like a lily-pad. The water came to her shoulders, and then, as she waded, her breasts, her waist. Weeds clung to her cuffs. She pushed through the rushes; ducks swam from her, startled. She wrapped her hand in the trailing branches of the willow and pulled herself up onto the bank. There she waited, flushed, dripping.

Yes: she had shamed him. Perhaps she knew it; she didn't look at him but instead out, across the water. Perhaps the others knew it too, because they looked meekly down at their feet and said nothing. He punted the ferry the remaining yards to the bank, and they stepped off without a word. He had not done anything wrong, and yet here he was, ashamed. That was the cunning power of girls, he thought. They turned a strong man weak. They made a good man penitent.

Back at the alehouse, he cradled his drink sullenly. His eye caught on the sides of his boots, powdered with fine dirt. The path was dry. Drier than last summer; he had needed to wash wet mud from them then. Already the water was low enough for the girl to wade, and it was only June. Not yet the height of the season, when the sun burned overhead and the river conceded to hard rock. It hadn't rained enough that year, not nearly enough. If the river dried up, the villagers could walk straight across the bed. No need for a ferryman then.

He thought about the girl. The way she waded, mocking him. The way her clothes had clung to her body. The way he'd pictured her in the water before she climbed in. Funny that: almost as though he had willed it into being. Perhaps he was more powerful after all, more favoured, more likely to pass through the gates of heaven. Yes. He took a sip of ale and smiled, liking the idea. That sounded right to him.

TWO

Summer was the season of strangeness. People behaved peculiarly then. Not just in the alehouse; people behaved peculiarly there year-round. Out in the wider world too. In the homes of Little Nettlebed, in the church and at the market—there were strangenesses all over. It was the heat that did it. It addled people's minds.

Temperance grew anxious in the summer. In winter, the villagers had their pint or two at cockshut, when the sun sank swiftly and the chickens were put in to roost, then hurried home in the dark. In summer, white evenings stretched interminably. People drank until they could not stand, heady after long haymaking days. Temperance was at her busiest then, serving drinks, mopping pools of vomit, prodding wan and wordless men out of the alehouse and into the road. A great thirst came over the men in the summer, a great greed. They were greedy for everything, even for her. Pinching, probing fingers found their way under her apron, stinking mouths pressed towards hers. It disturbed her, what the drink did to them.

The nickname—for Temperance was not the name she was

born with—had been given to her after she'd married John Shirly, the publican; it was then the men discovered her aversion to drink. She served it without difficulty but would not allow a drop to pass her lips. She could not kiss John after he'd been drinking, wouldn't even approach him. She hated to see how it changed him. It changed all men, every one of them. It had changed her father too—so much so that he, a careful man, a man who could navigate the local roads in a blindfold, tripped on a clear, moonlit night and hit his head. He bled to death, leaving his daughter with nothing. Fatherless, fearful. She wouldn't touch the poison that killed him. She wore hide gloves while serving ale; it appalled her to think of it seeping into her skin.

Yes, summer was the season of strangeness, and this summer, she felt, was stranger than others. There was Old Mother Mansfield's death, of course, although that in itself was no strange thing; she had been threatening to go for a long time. Enough to kill anybody, the strain of bringing up five girls, her dead son's daughters. She'd had a good death, people said, surrounded by her granddaughters, her husband, and her housemaids—an ideal end, in some ways. It's true that Mary, the youngest, had let out a curious cry after she passed, a kind of yelp, they said. But she was little, only six years old. To have seen so much death already—anyone would forgive her a brief, unseemly yelp.

The girls themselves had always seemed separate from the goings-on of the village, distant somehow. Their grandfather didn't like them to mingle, thinking perhaps that they were better than the people of Little Nettlebed. They went around in twos or threes, or very often all together. Dressed in black, now;

always unsmiling. It startled Temperance sometimes, coming across them in distant lanes or on the long river path in the day's dying hours. They haunted the borders of the village.

There had been other strangenesses. The vicar, absent from his pulpit for some weeks, had returned with a large velvet patch tied to the pink dome of his forehead. He was shooting, she heard, when his gun had burst, rupturing his skull. An extraordinary surgery had taken place then; the details nauseated Temperance, who didn't like to know about the inner workings of the body. Doctors bored into his skull to extract the splintered bone, and thereafter he wore a patch to conceal the hole. She'd asked her husband what he thought the hole looked like. He'd glanced at her and cleared his throat, as though the question made him uncomfortable, as though it was not the only thing he thought about during the sermon every Sunday. "It's not our business to know what the inside of the vicar looks like," he'd said. She pictured the hole like a quarry into the crust of the world; within was hell itself, all red and deep and sulphurous.

And then there was the fish: enormous and silver. That was the strangest thing of all.

It had been mid-afternoon; only Pete was in the alehouse at that time, staring out of the window. John was at the market, and Temperance was sweeping the floor. She relished the quiet of the alehouse before the men came in from their work. She felt safe during these moments; when it grew loud and busy, this feeling of safety lifted and hid itself elsewhere. Sometimes she would find, among the ash and mud she swept from the floor, a gleaming silver sixpence. Once she had even found a ring, which she slipped on sometimes, beneath the gloves she wore so as not to touch the ale.

She stopped sweeping and turned to Pete. "Fine weather we're having, aren't we?" she said.

She liked Pete, on the whole, despite his eccentricities. He drank too much, like the rest of them, and he spent too much time alone. Sometimes she saw him speaking to the swans. Occasionally, in warmer weather, he slept on his ferry or on the bank beside it. He had once thrown a tiny, writhing fish down his throat, like a goose. It was for the best, really, that he was to be married in a few weeks, although Temperance could not approve of his choice of bride. Agnes Bullock, the youngest daughter of a local merchant—too good for him in some ways, and in some ways far too bad. She was old, almost thirty, spoiled and silly. Temperance had heard things about her; she heard things about everyone. Gossip spread like mould in the alehouse's dank corners.

Pete glared at her. "Too hot," he said. "Wading weather."

She wasn't sure what he meant by this, but it didn't stop her from leaning on her broom and nodding. "Too much wading, and too much drinking. That's the problem with this place."

They looked at each other knowingly.

John burst in, his face flushed. "You're back early," Temperance said. "Did you pick up the chops?"

He shook his head, breath ragged. "Come, Temp," he said. "They've caught something. In the river. A miracle. A monster."

Temperance was used to John's exaggerations and generally dismissed them, but something in the wild look in his eyes, the colour in his cheeks, made her pause. A miracle? A monster? She wouldn't pass up the opportunity to see it. "Where?" she said.

"Across from the vicarage," he said. "Tubb, the schoolmaster, saw it. Sitting by the river, he was. Writing *poetry*."

He waited, allowing this bewildering detail to sink in.

"Saw something in the shallows, caught among the bulrushes." He swallowed. "A river monster. Big and bearded. Twice the size of a man."

Pete was on his feet. "Let's go," he said.

They left the alehouse, Pete ducking beneath the low lintel on which he'd often hit his head before, his body confounded after several pints. The sign swung above the door, the crudely painted swan rocking on its backdrop of rippled blue. Its creaking sound followed them across the Greater Nettlebed road and down the path through the meadows which flanked the river. The meadows stretched far, filled here with high grasses and the last of the cow parsley, and in the distance flattening where the cattle grazed. Beyond, hazy in the warm summer weather, stood the hill at Greater Nettlebed.

Temperance skipped to keep up with the others as they marched along the bank. She was short—the frothing cow parsley reached high above her head. Voices carried through the grass, and she arrived at last to find a crowd gathered by the sandy beach opposite the vicarage. She pressed through it, trying to catch her breath; around her, men and women muttered to each other, jostling. In the river stood Samuel Tubb and the young farmhand Robin Wildgoose. Like a jealous husband, Pete leapt in too: this watery stretch was his territory. "Where is it?" Temperance asked. "What is it?"

"They say it's a monster," someone answered. "Hard to tell from here. Giant, it looks like. Silver."

She pushed forward. She could see Robin's brown curls, his gentle face screwed into a frown. Samuel Tubb was shouting beside him. Pete's eyebrows rose; despite his weather-worn skin he seemed suddenly pale. Temperance pressed towards the beach to see what they were staring at. There it was, sides heaving, just as the others had described. A monster, ten or eleven feet long, its satin-shiny back stippled white and grey. It was as thick and muscular as a man's torso. From its face trailed long, white whiskers, twining and coiling like sea snakes. The monster was beached, it looked like, caught between unyielding bulrushes. She heard a whistle and saw, hovering in the clear blue sky, three waiting kites. They circled, watchful.

"Here," Pete was saying to Tubb and Robin. "Wrap your arms around it. Let's bring it in to the shore."

The three of them stood in a line beside the monster, their shirts rolled up to their elbows. They crouched together. There was a great thrashing, a lifting, the whipping back and forth of a long-finned tail. Mud was churned up from the riverbed, obscuring the monster and the men's arms, which cradled its broad body. Temperance saw that Pete's cheek was bleeding where something—perhaps the monster's rough back, which he'd pressed close to his face—had nicked it. "To the shore," he gasped, and the men, struggling with the wild and writhing creature, heaved it towards the beach.

The crowd, watching from the grass above, parted like water, while the kites settled in the branches of nearby trees. The men laid it down, first on the beach, in order to relieve their arms and backs, and then up on the grassy bank at the villagers' feet. Its sides puffed violently in and out, and it thrashed some more, its shiny back dusted in dirt.

"Unnatural," someone shouted. "Demon. Fetch the priest!"

"Not a demon," Pete said, kneeling beside the creature. He looked regretful, Temperance thought, as though he'd like to have seen a demon. "Just a sturgeon. A fish, that's all."

A fish—it rippled through the crowd. An enormous fish,

a bountiful find, a blessing. John stepped forward, beaming. "We'll take it up and cook it at the Swan!"

Temperance frowned. She pictured the bones, the charred skin and entrails, dropping all over her newly swept floor. "Wait," Pete said. "Sturgeon are royal fish—they belong to the crown. Half of it should be sent up to the King."

If people were disappointed by this, they didn't show it. It was decided. They would send the severed head and tail of the sturgeon to the King, and the rest would be served at the alehouse. It was a great day in Little Nettlebed, an auspicious day.

Temperance saw then among the crowd the five Mansfield sisters, their eyes shining with excitement. She thought, like her, like everyone there, that they were elated by the find and the prospect of a feast of fresh fish. It was only when she saw one of them—Hester, was it?—and then another—Mary, the youngest—rush forward to the vast, twitching body and try with feeble arms to roll it back into the water, that she realised they didn't share in the excitement at all. Instead, enraged by what had happened, they were actually trying to rob all these people of their meal and the King of his offering. She was glad when Pete pushed them out of the way, lifting a large boot and stamping down on the creature's head. The crowd gave out a small cheer, then fell immediately silent, awed by the size of it. Some men, John and Samuel Tubb among them, heaved the sturgeon onto their shoulders and made their way up the path like grinning pallbearers. The others followed, chattering with relief. They would be telling this tale for generations to come.

No one took much notice of the Mansfield girls, who hung back in a tight row. Hester was angrily tearful; Grace, always so anxious-looking, cradled her sister's waist. Without saying a word to Temperance, they set off down the path—away from the alehouse, the village, their home, and along the wending river.

Pete stayed to wash off his boot. He squinted at the girls. "They'd better be careful," he said quietly. "They need disciplining."

Temperance nodded. "Quite a thing, wasn't it," she said, drawing the outline of the creature in the dirt with her shoe. "The size of it!"

Pete grimaced. "That may be so," he said. "But it shouldn't have been beached. Just lying there among the rushes, a fine sturgeon like that. The river's too low." He scowled at the cloudless sky. "We need rain."

She looked up with him. The afternoon light cast the riverside in dreamlike colours, jaundicing the saucers of white flowers on the nearby elder, dipping the willow in gold. The cows glowed, watching her from the meadow in a silent ring, while delinquent hares leapt through the long orange grass. Birds screeched, and the river dallied, and in the far distance five black-clad sisters receded from sight. Below her, Pete washed the grease of the monstrous sturgeon from his foot.

The season of strangeness had begun.

THREE

The Thames hemmed Little Nettlebed like a green silk ribbon. Thomas stood at the bank and surveyed the village from across the water. Among the lilies, cygnets huddled clumsily in the wake of a pair of swans. Bands of tall bulrushes guarded the far bank, and beyond that stood trees and squat cottages and the blunt church tower. It was a pretty sight, but something about it troubled him. There were no people—none at all. No one was walking along the road or coming home from church. A wide wooden punt, tied to a stake below him, bumped dully against the rock.

He had passed an alehouse, and he walked up to it now to find the ferryman. From the river path, he crossed the road on which the coach had dropped him, the one coming from Greater Nettlebed. That had been a nice village—bigger than this one, and busier. Little Nettlebed seemed quiet, cut off from its surroundings by the river. He liked bustle and liveliness, but across the water everything looked green and still. A jackdaw chattered in a tree above him, and a chill crept up his arms.

He ducked into the alehouse, adjusting to the dim light within; it was like stepping into a warren, the beamed ceiling low, little doors leading to darkened rooms. The air smelled of ashes and ale. A woman was lugging a cask in gloved hands. "Here," Thomas said. "Let me help you."

She stood, looking at him. "Finally," she said, "a young man with manners."

Thomas heard scoffing in the corner and turned to see a man sitting in the inglenook window. He was tall and long-faced, with pale, red-rimmed eyes and a large mouth. He hunched a little, drawing his shoulders up around his ears. His hands, cradling a pint, were broad and blistered.

"Don't listen to her, lad," he said. "She's a sly one. She'll soon have you doing all the work around here, if you're not careful."

The woman tutted, but Thomas saw that she was smiling. He carried the cask to the far side of the room and straightened up, facing her. "I'm looking for the ferryman," he said. "My name's Thomas Mildmay. Joseph Mansfield has hired me to help with the haymaking."

The woman put her hands on her hips, watching him with interest. "Well, you've found your ferryman," she said, jerking her head towards the man. "That's Pete Darling. And I'm Temperance Shirly."

Thomas inclined his head, but the man made no movement to stand, sucking his hollowed cheeks and staring out of the window. "Working for Mansfield, you say?" he said.

Thomas followed the line of his sight out towards the river. "Yes."

"Let me finish my drink, then I'll ferry you across. Here, Temp, bring young Mildmay an ale, will you?"

Thomas sat down with the pint Temperance brought for him. He didn't want to be here. The ferryman, who had shifted his stare from the window to Thomas's face, had begun to worry him; he didn't like the way he gripped his tankard of ale, large hands wrapped tightly.

"Where are you from, boy?" Pete said.

"Milton," Thomas said. "Not far by coach."

"You left a family, a sweetheart?"

"Just my parents and my brothers."

"Ah." Pete belched quietly. "You'll miss them."

Thomas bristled. It bothered him, how much he missed them—his two brothers especially. They were like lungs to him, or teeth, or eyes. They were part of him. He realised, during the journey to Little Nettlebed, that he was changed without them. He felt lost. Men ought not to have such feelings, and—as his parents' eldest son—Thomas knew himself to be a man. "I'll be fine," he said gruffly.

Pete gave him an approving look. "I've no family myself," he said. "Just me and my father, it was, but he died several years ago."

"You won't be alone for much longer," Temperance called. "He's to be married next month," she said to Thomas.

Pete nodded, frowning.

"You've always lived here?" Thomas asked.

"Oh, yes," Pete said, his eyes back on the window. "Little Nettlebed's my home."

"Pretty place," Thomas said, taking a draught of his drink.

"Nowhere prettier." Pete's face softened. "Nice people too. On the whole."

He paused. Thomas wondered when he'd be permitted to cross the river.

"There are some to watch out for, of course," Pete continued.

Behind them, Temperance clicked her tongue.

"What?" Pete said. "The lad should know."

"Know what?" Thomas regretted the words as soon as he'd said them.

Pete passed a hand over his mouth and chin. Thomas saw him exchange a look with Temperance.

"The Mansfields, they like to keep themselves to themselves," he said at last.

Thomas gave a little shrug and finished his ale.

"No," Pete said, leaning closer. "You'll see. There's something about them. They aren't like other folk."

Thomas glanced at Temperance. She was looking at the floor, her mouth a tight knot.

"Listen," he said, getting to his feet. "I'd better not be late."

Pete rose, and Thomas followed him out of the alehouse. He was sorry to leave Temperance, who had, he felt, a settling influence on Pete. There was something almost elemental about this man; Thomas sensed that his mood might abruptly shift, like the sudden arrival of a storm on a calm day.

They stepped over clumps of hairy comfrey, flowers hanging like purple bells. Pete began untying his ferry, while Thomas watched on the bank behind him. In the shallow water, circling thick lily-pads, he found eyes and fidgeting forms—tadpoles turning into frogs. Some had stubby tails, others were dappled brown and green, caught in the border between different bodies. "Right," Pete said, stepping on the wooden platform. "Let's go."

Thomas joined him and, as Pete pushed off, thought about sitting. But no: it seemed girlish to sit. He would stand, his legs set apart for balance. In the river's green depths he found rippling weeds, the pearly glint of spent mussels, and, every so often, a quick, darting disturbance, something emerging from the dark bed. He dug his hands deep into his pockets. He didn't know how to swim.

"How'd you meet old Mansfield?" Pete asked.

"At the fair," Thomas said.

He had been there to find work, wearing red thread in his buttonhole to show that he was searching. The thread had caught the eye of a pretty girl—the way she looked at him made Thomas blush. She was with an old man, whom she brought across to meet him. *Let me get the measure of you*, the man had said. Thomas allowed him to reach out and appraise his shoulders, his arms, his legs, with seeing fingers.

"Were his granddaughters with him?" Pete said.

"There was a girl with him—maybe his granddaughter."

"Serious, sour-looking?"

"No," Thomas said, swallowing. "Pretty."

"That'll be the second one," Pete said. "There are five altogether."

Thomas said nothing. He was interested in hearing more about the five granddaughters, but not from Pete. The man spoke as though he were describing cuts of meat at the market.

"The eldest is the one you've got to watch out for—Anne. Prideful, that girl is. Nose in the air."

He pushed hard and continued. "Then there's the pretty one. She's haughty too, though not quite so bad. And then the youngest three. Wild bunch, no discipline at all."

He pressed again on the pole, and they jerked forward. "They do what they like, the Mansfield sisters. No one ever stops them. Rude, they are—you'd struggle to get a word of greeting from them. And grasping. Once I found them picking cockles in the river—a good haul they got—and they didn't offer me a single one. Not one. Guarded that basket as though I was going to rob them."

Thomas could see how it offended him, the idea that he might want something from the girls.

"They roam around the village like lords," Pete continued. "Anytime they please, even well into the evening, without a thought for properness." He paused. "They deserve whatever comes their way."

He was like a bloodhound which had found its scent. His face reddened, his punts became harder and more frequent. He grew short of breath. Thomas didn't know why these girls enraged him so much; they weren't even women, no trouble to him at all. Thomas himself had never found anything of interest in the opposite sex, for the most part, nothing to be excited or bothered by. Girls simply weren't worth his time.

The boat reached the far bank, nudging through the stems of towering yellow irises that grew in the shallows. Thomas leapt off, glad to be back on land.

"Thanks," he said, inclining his head.

Pete leaned on his pole. "Be careful, lad. You hear me? Mind yourself around them."

Thomas nodded and made his way up the path. Glancing back, he found that he was being watched, and the feeling of the ferryman's eyes on him persisted as he pressed beyond the trees. On the road, he realised he didn't know where he was going and could see no one to ask. A hen scratched at the shrubs by his feet. In a nearby cottage, someone sang a mournful tune. The smell of roasting fat reached him, and he discovered he was hungry. He kept walking, hoping he would soon find his way to the farm. The ferry was far behind him now, but he still sensed, somehow, that his every move was being marked.

The sun was beginning to grow hot. He heard voices and

looked up to see a narrow path to his right, fringed with cow parsley and bitter dock, down which two boys were walking. They were clearly brothers: one nearing Thomas's age, the other younger, both brown-haired, their skin generously freckled. Thomas felt a pang when he saw them. Their faces were alike, as was the way they held themselves; they passed their hands over the flowers and grasses beside the path, allowing the leaves to tickle their palms as they walked. Thomas thought of his own brothers—together right now, walking along a similar path, perhaps.

"Good day," he called, and the brothers fell silent, looking at him.

The younger boy rubbed his nose. "Good day," he said.

"Shush, Richard," said the older one, stepping forward. "Let me speak."

"My name's Thomas Mildmay," Thomas said. "I'm looking for the Mansfields' farm."

"You're nearly there," the boy said. "It's the house up the road on the right. You can't miss it." He looked uncertain. "I'm Robin, by the way. This is Richard."

"Thank you," Thomas said. "I lost my way and didn't come across anyone to ask. This place is quite lifeless, isn't it? I haven't seen a soul since the ferry."

"It's market day," the younger boy, Richard, said seriously. "They're all at the market. But don't worry—if it's loudness you like, you'll be just fine. The villagers can get very loud."

Thomas nodded. Even deafening loudness seemed preferable to this.

"You're here for the haymaking," Robin said.

"Yes," Thomas said, although he wasn't sure he'd been asked a question.

"I'll be working on Mansfield's land too."

"Ah," Thomas said. "I'll see you soon, then."

He walked away, lifting his hand. The brothers said nothing in parting; Richard picked his teeth. Despite their reserve, Thomas found something he liked in the pair. The village's oppressive atmosphere—the way it watched, its rankling quiet—seemed to lift a little in their company.

He found the house along the road, just as Robin had described. His first impression was of abundance. Everywhere he looked was urgent fruitfulness: dog roses blooming around the door, foxgloves pressing up against the walls, a kitchen garden choked with carrots, lettuces, and climbing beans. A cow was tied to the fence, its udders veined and straining. Six white kittens played in the lush border nearby.

No one appeared, and Thomas trudged up to the yard, hesitant. The quiet that had overcome the village seemed to have infected this place too. There was no sign of the old man, or of the girls, or any maids. It was as though the huge farmhouse and wanton garden were concealing them somewhere in their depths.

He looked up then—why, he didn't know—and found that he was being observed. He had imagined hidden eyes on him earlier, but now the feeling was made real. A face was watching him from one of the higher windows: pale, framed by dark hair. It vanished as soon as he saw it. The foreboding that had troubled him on the ferry returned to him. This place, this village, looked just as his own did, but there seemed to be something unnatural here. It hung in the stifling air. It lingered behind windows, watchful. He took off his cap and screwed it into a ball.

At last, a girl came out into the yard. "Come this way,

please," she called and, without stopping, stepped back into the house.

It was the pretty girl from the fair, Mansfield's second granddaughter. She was a few years younger than him, fifteen, perhaps, with blue eyes and conker-brown hair. This was not the girl from the window; this girl was softer, smiling. The other girl had seemed somehow older, and harder. The watching girl had wished him ill.

"It's Thomas, isn't it?" the girl said when he reached the door. "I'm Elizabeth."

He nodded. "Pleased to meet you, Miss Elizabeth."

"Come and have some food, then Connie will show you to your room."

He followed her along the passage into a wide, wood-panelled hall. Dark beams lined a high ceiling, and daylight battled through narrow windows. On the walls hung finely painted cloths, a sea of foaming greens and fruit and flowers. Three girls were standing by a long table. "Here," she said, "these are my younger sisters, Hester, Grace, and Mary."

The girls all had the same dark hair and pale blue eyes. He nodded at each of them and twisted his cap in his hand. Hester grinned at him, and he felt grateful for her warmth, although within the smile he thought he found a seam of mockery. Her face was freckled, and her hair was shorter than her sisters'. Dirt varnished each of her fingernails. He judged her to be the age of his youngest brother, newly thirteen; they shared the swaggering air of fresh-sprung adolescence. The girl beside her, Grace—a couple of years younger—could barely raise her eyes to look at him, her mouth puckering tightly. Mary was only about six, gaping wordlessly up at him. One of her front teeth was missing; the gap was bloody and raw.

The old man walked in from the far door, his hand on the shoulder of a fifth girl. This was the face—the watching face. Thomas looked away.

"Grandfather," Elizabeth said. "The boy has arrived."

Thomas flinched at this—he was no boy. But perhaps in this place, inhabited by girls, the language of manhood was rarely spoken. He didn't consider Mansfield a real man, not enough to teach these girls what true manliness was. He was old, for a start, muscle withering to papery skin. And he was almost blind, made reliant on his granddaughters and maidservants, on his own thin hands, to see.

"Ah, Mildmay," the old man said, and Thomas approached. "Welcome."

Mansfield's eyes gleamed in the dim light of the hall, white and filmy like floating planets. "I trust you had a pleasant journey?"

"Very pleasant, thank you, sir."

"Good. Sit down and have some dinner."

He could sense the girl watching him but didn't dare look at her. "This is Anne, my eldest granddaughter."

He gave her a jerky bow and at last raised his eyes to her face. It was an unusual face. More unusual up close than it had first appeared at the window: thin and pale and somehow ancient, although he could see she must be his own age. Her expression was guarded, in the way that older faces get, not so open, not so eager, but withdrawn into itself. Her chin seemed to lift a little, as if in defiance. She examined him unblinkingly.

Elizabeth's prettiness had made him awkward, but in the presence of Anne he became something much worse. He forgot how to move. The air encasing his body became thick like mud, binding him. He could barely breathe, yet while his limbs became sluggish and slow, his thoughts quickened. Something happened to him when he saw her. A feeling came to him that he had only experienced twice before. (Once when the farmer in his village had let him rescue the runt of a litter, destined for drowning; the other when the local pond had frozen over during a bitter winter frost and he'd skated clean across it.) The feeling was of triumph, and brilliance, and total, blissful possession. It felt like ruling and serving simultaneously.

He couldn't explain it. He saw before him a plain girl, unexceptional in almost every way, but when his eyes met hers his insides leapt like a salmon and his body stopped working. He was amazed by her, and ashamed of his amazement. He dropped his cap. His ears burned.

She shuffled with the old man to the table. Through the door came two maidservants, carrying food on earthenware dishes. "Very good," Mansfield said. "Thank you, Connie. Thank you, Amie."

Connie and Amie—sisters, Thomas assumed from the shared squareness of their faces, the same golden hair wisping beneath their caps—frowned at him, but no one bothered to introduce them. The girls were serving the food, talking softly and excitedly about their mornings, tending to their grandfather. There was nowhere to eat apart from the long, dark table around which they all now sat, including the maids. Thomas perched himself on the bench, as far as possible from the Mansfields.

"Mutton again!" Hester said, pulling a plate towards her. "That makes four days in a row."

Elizabeth tapped her sister on the hand. "You're lucky to have it. Here, pass Mary these turnips—nice and soft for your sore gums."

The little one scowled, then gave the others a superior look. "I found a toad this morning—it's in my pocket."

"No toads at the table," the girl beside her—Grace—said primly. "Anne, I did the needlework you asked for. You better be pleased—I pricked my finger."

"Barely a scratch," said Hester, glancing over. "I saw a man at the market without any fingers at all. Maybe a wolf got him. Or maybe he lost them in a wager."

"Maybe it's no concern of yours what happened to the poor man's fingers," Elizabeth said. "Be quiet and eat your mutton."

The girls ate quickly, ravenously. Thomas watched them with wonder and disgust—Anne especially. He saw how blood from the meat trickled down their chins, how vinegar and grease collected at the corners of their mouths. He listened to them talk—murmuring asides to each other, swallowing shrieks of laughter. The old man sat among them, saying little, staring. Nearest to Thomas, the maids didn't speak at all, although the younger one, Amie, smiled every so often at something the girls had said. She seemed gentler than her sister, who let out loud sighs at intervals, as though finding this meal, this earth, this very life, intolerably tiresome. Connie was pretty, Thomas thought, in a golden-haired, soft-figured sort of way, but she didn't match the loveliness of Elizabeth. Amie had a pleasing face, despite it being pitted with the kind of pockmarks common in those who had lived in cities. Hester, the third Mansfield sister, was too boyish, but the younger girls, Grace and Mary, might grow up to be nice-looking someday. Of all of them, Thomas thought, surveying them with burgeoning connoisseurship, Anne was probably the ugliest. But she was the one he kept looking at.

Thomas was unacquainted with the world of girls. He had no sisters, only his two younger brothers, who would soon, like him, be sent off to work. He was used to short-haired, fuzzy-cheeked, belching, farting, strong-armed boys. Girls were boring: this was something he and his brothers had always understood. They were slower and weaker and didn't know how to take jokes. He'd been taught to believe that girls—especially ones who lived in a house like this—should be elegant and quiet, their laughs like musical instruments, their hands plump and clean. These girls weren't like that at all. They were funny and loud. Their laughter came in shouts. He was enchanted by them, even over the space of a single meal.

The way they held themselves, the whispering folds of their dresses, their habit of tucking their hair behind their ears—it was at once both fascinating and foreign. Last year he had seen for the first time a bear being baited at a tavern in town, and he felt now a little as he had then. He'd marvelled to encounter the creature up close: its greasy fur and persistent scent, the pink of its tongue, the chain biting into its neck. The bear had left him light-headed, and these girls had done the same. He was glad when the meal was cleared away and Connie showed him to his living quarters—not in the house but outside, next to the stable. From his window he could see the back of the building, the high windows where he supposed the sisters slept. He wondered if, at night, he would be able to hear them talking.

"Nice family," Connie told him confidentially as she showed him his room. "Though not everyone in the village is so fond of them as I am. When people were starving hungry in this county—you recall, when bread got costly—"

Thomas nodded.

"Master Mansfield made a fine penny selling flour then. That was a few years ago now, but some people haven't forgotten. Still, Old Mother Mansfield—that's what people called her—and Master Mansfield, they've always been kind to me and Amie. She even remembered us in her will. Very good of her, it was."

She lingered, although the tour of his small room was long over. "The girls . . . Well, you'll soon see. They're not ordinary girls. Both parents dead, of course. Their mother died giving birth to Mary. The father went soon afterwards. Coach accident, very unfortunate. It's little wonder the girls are . . . as they are."

Thomas couldn't help himself. "As they are?"

Connie smiled, gratified. She clearly appreciated an audience.

"Oh, you'll see. They have their funny ways."

He nodded again, not understanding.

She was still smiling. "I'll take my leave."

He was glad when she left. Her words worried him. He took a steadying breath, then stepped out again into the sunlit yard. He passed chickens and a strutting cockerel, beds of swaying flowers, the tethered cow. He had been taken on to help with the haymaking, but until it began he didn't know what the old man intended him to do. He kicked a stone idly and stuffed his hands into his pockets.

Something sounded at the side of the building, a clattering just out of sight. He rounded the corner and found by the kitchen door a low, bricked well into which a girl was leaning. For a moment he did nothing, before stepping up beside her to the lip of the well. "May I help you, miss?"

The girl half turned her face to him, her body still folded. It was Hester, the boyish one. She looked at him with disdain. "Oh," she said. "It's you."

She turned back to the well, her hands outstretched below her.

"May I help you?" he said again, this time peering over. Far below he saw the glimmer of disturbed water.

She looked up from the rope she was holding. "Quick, then. One of the kittens was playing with the rope and has fallen in. My sisters will be devastated."

He swallowed. He couldn't let the girls be devastated. He grabbed the rope from her and pulled, but the bucket was empty, the gathered water swimming and clear. "I'll go in," he said.

She observed him, blue eyes watchful. "Yes," she said. "You should go in."

Madness, to follow a kitten into a well. Yet here he was, desperate to please these sisters he'd only just met. He lowered himself down the rope, ignoring his burning palms and the scuffing of his only pair of shoes along the brick. Hester's head was contoured against the sky.

"It isn't deep," she said.

She was right; he quickly reached the water, and in the water he found that he could stand. He fumbled about, breathless, dreading. Despite the heat of the day, the water was cold, and he could feel his jaw beginning to shake. His fingers swept icy corners. Looking up, he caught the girl's bright stare. "I'm sorry," he said. "I can't find it."

She observed him a little while longer, then made a sound like a snicker and walked away. No, he thought, scowling at the circle of blue sky above him. Surely not—? He began heaving himself up by the rope, feet scrabbling on slick patches of moss. For a moment—a brief, abasing moment—he thought he might be trapped down there forever, and a scream rose threateningly in his throat. But at last he reached the mouth of the well and emerged with his heart hammering in his ears, casting an angry look at the upper windows of the house. Did the sisters care if he freed himself? Were they all assembled there, looking down on him and laughing? The glare on the glass obscured them from view. Later, drying himself in the sun, he saw a line of six white kittens tumble past. They looked fine—pouncing, playful. He remembered then what Connie had told him about the girls, and the ferryman's warning too. Perhaps there was some wisdom in what they said.

FOUR

Joseph Mansfield entered each day nose first. Before getting out of bed, he inhaled deeply, acquainting himself with the morning through the smells it presented to him. He found it a useful augury. So much of what lay ahead could be discovered in the air: in its stillness, in its dryness.

Today, he could smell the lingering scent of the tallow candle he kept by his bed—greasy, meaty, working its way into his pillows and coverlets. This was a constant smell, the base note of his day. Beyond that, the first curling tendrils of woodsmoke reached him from the fire in the kitchen. Scents from the garden crowded in at the open window: roses rambling up the side of the house, fruit ripening in the orchard, hay heaped in the stable-yard, the distant reek of the pigs.

And there was something else. He breathed it in. This smell was dusty and brittle; it smelled . . . He paused, considering it. Yes, he thought, it smelled like lack. Usually, he could find—somewhere in the morning air—the sweet fragrance of dew. He could almost see it, pooling in cupped leaves, caressing stalks and petals, clear and moist. But today there was no note of moisture. It was unusual, at this time of year—an absence.

He opened his eyes. Before him was the blur of his bed-hangings, and the crack of white dawn light. He swung his legs around, planting his feet on the wooden boards. Since his sight had deteriorated, detail had forsaken him. He had forgone clarity in favour of loose shapes and colours. Amie laid out his clothes, which he now found on the chest by his bed. When all was as it should be, he did just fine.

But after his wife's death, all had not been as it should be. Those were dark, disrupted days, when the order Mansfield coveted was unpicked like a thread, the beloved pattern unravelling. What was he without her? She was the foundation on which their family was built, its brickwork, its bone. Without her, he was lost. His eyes troubled him more than ever before.

Groping his way downstairs, he made for the little parlour where he and Anne met each morning. There she was, stirring the ill-smelling tincture. "Morning, Grandfather," she said, and kissed him on the cheek.

He felt for the chair and sat. "Good morning, Anne. Have you brought my beer?"

"Here," she said, placing the cup in his hand.

He drank. The beer had been prescribed to help with dryness in his brain, believed to be affecting his sight. He could feel the liquid lubricating his mind.

He set the cup down, and she stepped forward with the eyewash. She was a good girl, perhaps his favourite. When his wife died, she had taken on so many tasks without complaint. She was a mother to her sisters, and she helped him manage the household. He didn't know what he would do without her. He reached out and found her hand.

"How are you, my dear?"

"I'm well, thank you."

She brought her hand up to the back of his head and tilted his face to the ceiling.

"How are you finding the new boy?" he said.

She began trickling the tincture into his eye, and he flinched, as he always did. This too had been prescribed to clear his sight, an eyewash of sulphur, turpentine, honey, rose water, and eyebright. His nostrils sought out each of the ingredients. His eyes began to stream.

"I'm sure he'll be a great help to you with the haymaking," she said.

"I hope so. He seems like a good lad. He'll work around the yard and in the garden until haymaking starts." He paused, wincing, as she began washing his other eye. "He'll help you and your sisters."

She wiped his cheeks with a piece of linen. "We don't need help, Grandfather."

He tried to focus on her. It saddened him that the details of her face, all their faces, were lost to him now. He had memories of their expressions—smiles, frowns, quick glances—which he overlaid onto their blurred features. But they were growing up: the pink cheeks, the laughing looks, were sure to have matured into something more refined, something he would never see.

Anne saddened him the most. As a child, she had been the twin image of her father in his boyhood. Dark brown curls crowning a pale, pointed face, little mouth in a constant pout. Like her father, she had always been more solemn than other children. She contained experience beyond her years. She seemed to know about hardship, how it crept into one's life like a cuckoo, casting out happiness forever. Happiness was frail and flimsy: a petal, a whisper. Hardship was constant. It was muscular and loud. Only fools forgot this vital fact, her face explained. Only fools failed to let it guide their every waking thought and deed.

Yes, she was his strength. And although he could no longer clearly see her expression, he could still read her. He felt the unhurried way she washed his eyes, the gentle hand at the back of his head, and found that she was relaxed today; she was not always so relaxed. He heard, as she bent over the table, gathering the things, the suggestion of humming. Something was different this morning. The knots within her were loosening.

He thought about this over breakfast, barely listening to the chatter of the girls around him. The maids left the table, but he didn't move. Chewing on a bit of bread, he turned his attention to his granddaughters. He could hear Hester dictating a game by the fire—Elizabeth and Grace were with her.

"Flatten the ashes—go on, with your hand. It's not hot any more."

He could hear the pleasure in her voice; she enjoyed the role of ringleader.

"Go on, Lizzie," she said. "Don't be so precious. You've got to get your hand dirty."

"Like this?" Grace asked.

"Very good. Now take this twig and draw a line, and I'll tell you what the line has to say about you."

"Fortune-telling?"

Grace again—she liked to know she was getting it right.

"Exactly."

"Oh, Hester, go on, let me play," Mary said from the table.

"There's only enough space for three," Hester said coldly.

There must have been some sort of falling out. Joseph could never keep up with their shifting allegiances.

"Excellent," he heard Hester say. "Now let me take a look at them."

There was shuffling and smothered laughter.

"Interesting," Hester said, and Joseph imagined her stroking her chin, aping the wise men of Oxford—once a favourite game of hers. "Your line is clear, Elizabeth." She drew a breath. "You'll marry a pauper, but you'll be very happy together and will have six charming children."

Joseph heard Elizabeth huff and stand.

"Grace, yours is a little harder to read. It looks as though you'll have renown in your lifetime. People will hear all about your goodness and travel for miles to see you."

He pictured Grace's reddening cheeks.

"Oh, please, Hester," Mary said beside him. "I'm very sorry about your dress. Please can I have a turn?"

Joseph finished his bread and washed it down with more beer. He should go—there was work to be done. But he liked hearing the girls and their games.

"Fine," Hester said. "Come here, Mary. You too, Anne—everyone has to do it now."

Mary clattered across the hall. He heard Anne move towards the fireplace.

"Don't try to influence it," Grace murmured to Mary. "Just draw whatever line you like."

"Now this is interesting," Hester said. He could hear her grinning. "Mary's going to see the world. She'll sail on a large ship, a galleon with big white sails, and she'll go absolutely everywhere. All the way up the Thames to London. Even across to France!"

Joseph listened to Mary wriggling with delight and smiled.

"But Anne," Hester continued, her voice serious, "yours is

a different story." She stopped. "You'll fall in love," she said at last, "but the love will be brief."

She paused again.

"There's something else here. Something . . ." She cleared her throat. "You're going to be hunted. You're going to be afraid."

Joseph heard her throw the twigs into the fireplace. Her voice was quiet. "It's a silly game. Nonsense, you know."

He pushed himself to his feet. "Nonsense, as you say, Hester," he said. "No more fortune-telling today. I think everyone's got more important things to be getting on with."

He searched the silent hall for any sound from Anne, but she said nothing. He tried to smile at her, hoping to convince her that all would be well, that she shouldn't be troubled by Hester's game, but he couldn't find her in the dim light. The shape of her had vanished; it was as though she had disappeared into the walls.

The morning was calling, and he left the girls, feeling his way out of the house and across the yard. Worry gathered like pooling water in his mind. He worried constantly about his granddaughters, in a way that he'd never worried about his son. Were they happy? Were they safe? His wife had left him with an impossible task: to protect the girls from the hazardous world, a ravenous world, a world with teeth. Joseph alone was no match for it, and the girls had no interest in helping him. They wanted to live—loudly, freely. All of them, even little Mary, even nervous Grace and unlaughing Anne. He could hear it in the way they spoke about the village. It was in the walks they took along the river. Their love of the market. Their longing to see London.

He had worked hard to make their home a place of plenty.

They wouldn't want for anything here. They could learn to read, they could play. But the world outside the garden wall seemed to interest them more than any lesson or game he could devise. He attempted to set limits, to insist on rules, but they broke them so often that he'd had to give up, knowing, anyway, that his wife would have hated the thought of him making their world somehow smaller—she'd always resolved to do the opposite. So he tried instead to trust the girls, and every day he awaited misfortune.

He passed the dovecote, listening to the cooing, the soft fluttering, within. A little way off he could hear the hives, and around him the muttering hens. He allowed himself to be guided by the sound of the cow rubbing her rump against the gate. In his own house and garden he was as quick as a sighted man. Nothing escaped him; he found his footing surely. He arrived at the stone wall at the end of the kitchen garden and reached out, feeling it with subtle fingers. Finding the gate, he walked around to the other side of the wall and felt it again, measuring the way the stones fit into each other. "Good," he murmured to himself. He had asked Mildmay to mend the wall, and the young man had done so satisfactorily.

Just as he was about to return to the garden, he paused. A foul smell carried on the air. Something was rotting or dying nearby, very near, here, by his feet. He stooped to the ground by the gate. His fingers found a sharpness, another sharpness, a row of small, fierce sharpnesses like knives lined up for battle. The sharpnesses continued for several feet, snaking along the grass outside his garden. They ended abruptly in a stump. And now here was the source of the smell: long slippery ropes, tossed onto the dirt. His granddaughters had told him about the giant fish they had seen on the bank; its spine and insides had seemingly been dumped outside his gate. But why? And by whom?

He thought then that he could hear something behind him—stifled laughter, it sounded like, or perhaps just the breeze-rustled branches. He stood up and turned towards the sound but could see nothing but the blurred outline of the trees. Wiping his fingers on a handkerchief, he pulled himself up to his full height and returned to his place of safety within the wall, leaving the entrails and the bones behind him.

FIVE

Pete's thoughts always found their way back to heaven. It occupied him constantly—when he was working, when he was drinking, when he was drifting off to sleep. He liked to think that it shared a landscape with Oxfordshire. There too a wide, willow-fringed river flowed through green meadows, looping round gentle hills. Flowers abounded, and food was plentiful. Animals frolicked in the shade of ancient trees. His mother had made heaven her home; he hoped one day to join her.

It bothered him, sometimes, to think that his road to heaven was not without obstacles. There were one or two things standing in his way, troubling little sins that he hoped the saints would find it in themselves to forgive. He knew by heart the wickednesses that might prevent him from entering the kingdom of God; he recited St. Paul's list to himself often, muttering it under his breath as he walked. *Adultery, fornication, uncleanness, lasciviousness, idolatry, witchcraft, hatred, variance, emulations, wrath, strife, seditions, heresies, envyings, murders, drunkenness, and revellings.* Seventeen sins in total. Of these, he was most guilty of drunkenness. He often drank more than he should, particularly when traffic across the river was quiet and he had nothing else to occupy him. He regularly resolved to drink less but would wake on the riverbank at dawn regardless, his head aching, his spirit aggrieved.

Drunkenness was his most frequent sin, but it wasn't the worst. Every man in England was guilty of drunkenness. He felt guiltier about the hatred, and about the uncleanness. These were sins he had never confessed to, that no one else knew about; they polluted his mind in private. The uncleanness had crept up on him in his youth—a suggestion, an idea. He buried it, ashamed, but the idea kept returning to him. It involved his body, and another's. It involved—no, he wouldn't even think it. It flourished like river weed when he gave it his attention. Much better to suppress it until his nuptials next month. Then he wouldn't need to worry. Everyone knew that marriage was like laundering—it made the unclean clean.

Hatred presented a bigger problem. There was no solution for the hatred which tormented him every day. He hated anything weaker than himself—women, children, sometimes even animals. Soft men troubled him too. But really, it was women he hated the most. He hated how slow they were, how physically incapable, how stupid. He hated their incompleteness, their cunning, and their lust. He saw the way they looked at him. They tempted him into uncleanness.

The worst type of women were the ones who didn't know their place in the order of things. There seemed to be a lot of them around nowadays, women who thought themselves superior, who'd forsaken nice, feminine qualities like meekness and humility. Something terrible happened to him in the presence of such women. A rage descended, a desire to punish. He remembered the feeling of keeping the Mansfield sisters captive on his ferry for that fleeting moment, before Anne lowered herself into the river. How pleasing it had been to control their fate, however briefly. Sometimes he convinced himself that it wasn't really a sin at all, this punishing urge, that in fact he was acting according to God's will, despising women for the crime Eve had committed. In his heart, however, he knew this wasn't true, that hatred was hatred, and that he, Pete Darling, was the greatest hater of all.

He looked up and saw, over the water, old Joseph Mansfield waving his hat. Beside him was one of his granddaughters—from this distance, Pete couldn't make out which one she was. He punted across the river, observing the pair. Mansfield, once tall, was beginning to hunch from years of farm labour. He had an eerie knack of gazing intently, as though he could see. Next to him, the girl was watching Pete; her challenging stare told him it was the eldest sister. She believed herself to be better than him, that was what he'd come to understand. The look she gave him sent violence coursing through his body. It made him want to do unmentionable things. It made him want to—

"There you are, Darling," the old man said as the ferry met the edge of the bank. "Take this. We're going over to the Swan."

Pete took the coins Mansfield handed him. He didn't look at the girl. There was devilry in her; just to look at her would corrupt him somehow. She even smelled like the devil. In her arms was a basket filled with fish guts and bones. He turned away, disgusted.

Anne and the old man said nothing as he punted them across. The silence felt to Pete like a slight. Once again, the Mansfields were too good to speak to him—that's what the silence said. He and his boat were just a method of travel, like a horse or their own feet. He was determined that they treat him with more dignity.

"What takes you to the alehouse today, then, sir?" he asked, pushing on the pole.

Mansfield made a clicking noise with his tongue. "I have business with the publican."

"Very good, sir," Darling said. He paused. "It's been busy, you know, the ferry. Much busier than I've ever seen it."

This wasn't true. He wasn't sure why he'd said it, except that he didn't want Mansfield and his granddaughter to pity him. He wanted them to think he had plenty of work. He wanted them to look on him as someone who was flourishing, to whom life had been good. In fact, he thought, looking up at the sky, he feared that the opposite was true. There'd been no rain for a few weeks now. Soon the river would start shrinking.

"Wait here, will you, Darling?" Mansfield said, stepping off the boat at the far bank. "We won't be long."

Pete watched them walk away. The sun winked at him on Anne's satin hair. She hadn't spoken a word during the ferry ride over.

He idled on the bank, watching dragonflies hover by the bulrushes. It was growing hot again, and he thought about going up to the Swan for a drink but soon decided not to; he didn't want the Mansfields thinking he'd followed them there. He would wait until he'd ferried them back.

Someone was approaching; he heard rustling behind him. He turned to see Robin Wildgoose walking through the crisping cow parsley. Pete had known Robin all his life, but the boy wasn't much to his liking. His manner bothered Pete—he was too mild, too quiveringly earnest. He worked in the fields and went to the alehouse, but Pete often felt he didn't like to be among other men. He seemed more comfortable in the company of women.

Robin looked up and saw him staring, and Pete made out a blushing in the boy's cheek. "Coming from the alehouse, are you?" he said, standing.

"Just dropping something off with Temperance," Robin mumbled.

Pete raised an eyebrow. So the lad's father had sent his girlish son to pay his drinking debts.

"Hoping to cross?"

"Yes," Robin said, looking at his feet.

"Wait a little, won't you? Then I can take you over with the Mansfields."

Robin looked momentarily alarmed, troubled, perhaps, by the idea of waiting here with Pete. Pete spat in the clover and stuck his hands in his pockets.

"Did you see them up there? The old man and his granddaughter?"

Robin nodded.

"What were they doing?"

Robin looked up at him, wide-eyed. "Mansfield's angry because the remains of that sturgeon were dumped outside his house. He thinks John Shirly meant to insult him."

Pete's eyebrows lifted. "What did Shirly say?"

"He denied it."

Pete grimaced and stared out across the water. "Some could say the Mansfields had it coming."

Robin was silent.

"They've made a lot of enemies in Little Nettlebed," Pete said. He could feel Robin flinch beside him. "Still," he continued, enjoying the boy's discomfort, "we'll all get our just deserts, when the time comes."

Side by side, they eyed the river, tracing the curves of the current in the water. "It'll be haymaking soon," Pete said. "Are you working on Mansfield's land again this year?"

"Yes," Robin said, still watching the water.

Pete knew he should stop. He had said enough about the Mansfields—Robin would think him obsessed. But in that moment he did feel obsessed. The Mansfield sisters had taken possession of his mind, turning him away from God, towards hatred and uncleanness.

"You ever see Mansfield's granddaughters?"

He saw Robin glance at him. "Sometimes."

"Queer girls, aren't they?"

Robin was silent.

"The other day, the eldest one—" He stopped and swallowed, as though girding himself to say her name. "Anne. She got clean in the river while I was ferrying them across. Waded through the water as though it was nothing."

He was gratified to see Robin's eyebrows rise.

"They're odd, I tell you. Always have been."

Robin was blushing again, which Pete took to mean he disagreed with what was being said but was too afraid to say so. The boy's meekness irritated him. He felt the familiar anger rising, a pricking need to humiliate. He was just about to speak when the gate clattered shut behind them; Mansfield and Anne were approaching. The basket of fish guts was gone.

"We'll go back now, Darling," Mansfield called, forging through the long grass.

Pete wondered with a gleeful kind of curiosity if the old man would know where the bank ended and the river began or if he'd watch him stride straight into the water. He was almost disappointed when Mansfield stopped just short of the river's edge. It was impossible to know how much he could see.

"Of course," he murmured and began untying the ferry.

He offered his hand to help Anne down, but she didn't take it. "How's your mother, Robin?" she asked when they were on their way. "And your brother? He's not with you today—you're usually together, I think."

Robin pinkened. "They're well, thank you, Miss Anne. I was just visiting the alehouse—my mother doesn't like Richard to go there. Too young, she says."

His face looked almost wistful.

"And her back—any better?"

Pete scowled. Anne Mansfield had no interest in Robin's mother's back. The only interest Anne Mansfield had was in proving to Pete that he was not worthy of her time. She was playing games with him, and he hated it.

"A little, thank you, miss." Robin paused and looked down at his hands. "It's the pillow lace; it's hard work."

"I'm grieved to hear it," Anne said.

But she wasn't, Pete knew. None of the Mansfields had ever been grieved by the troubles of their neighbours.

An eel rose to the surface near the ferry, and they stopped talking, watching its speckled back carve through the water. Steadied by Anne's hand on his arm, Mansfield stood, squinting at the distant willows. Pete wondered if he'd found what he was looking for at the alehouse. He knew the Shirlys hadn't done it—tipped those entrails outside Mansfield's farm—but perhaps they'd apologised anyway, to soothe the old man's smarting pride.

At the far side, he strode to the front of the ferry and held up his arm for Mansfield, who gripped it, heaving himself onto the bank. He turned back and held out his hand for Anne, allowing a grin to flicker across his face: she couldn't pass without taking it. For a moment, she did nothing, looking at his outstretched hand as though it were something disgusting—frogspawn, her face said, or giblets. He felt his fingers begin to tremble, rage surging through him; he feared that he would slap her. Her eyes closed briefly, and she took his hand at last, stepping onto the bank. And then she was gone, walking briskly behind her grandfather.

Robin muttered something and hurried away, and Pete was alone with the hand that had touched Anne Mansfield. He cradled it in his other arm; it felt heavy and hot. He thought he'd got the better of her, but he was wrong: the touch of her hand had unleashed more hatred and uncleanness than he'd ever known before. It was all he could think about—nothing on that quiet summer's day could dispel it. His thoughts about Anne Mansfield were as hot as hellfire; he could feel them burning inside him. It would take a lot of drink to put that burning out.

SIX

ROBIN WILDGOOSE WAS NOT LIKE OTHER MEN: THIS WAS made plain to him early in life, and he had been reminded of it most days since. He did not have the appetites that they had. Others believed they had the God-given right for their demands to be met, their greed satisfied, but Robin didn't share this view. He made no claims on the world; it owed him nothing.

He was gentle in a way that troubled his mother and disgusted his father, who made it clear he hoped for more from Richard, his second son, praising him for his strength, punishing Robin for his softness. Robin understood this but didn't seem able to change; the facts of himself were set in stone. For instance, he had always shown an unusual affection for animals. Once, looking for a quiet place to be alone, he had climbed among the roosting chickens and—warmed by their nestled bodies—fallen soundly asleep. He thought about that often, the refreshing rest he'd had there, the feathers and the shit that had clung to his clothes, the way his father, furious and vengeful, had made him wring one of their necks for dinner. The village was full of violence of this sort. Dogs were booted and smacked; rabbits were skinned; pigs were spit-roasted whole, their faces frozen in sad, watchful smiles. Robin fantasised about living one day in a large house filled with the partridges and rabbits and pigs and geese that he'd rescued from the plates of hungry men.

When he was among them, the hungry men, he had learned as best he could to disguise his gentleness. It was a matter of mimicking what he heard them say, of copying their mannerisms. Some of them were God-fearing, but their main god, the one at whose temple they worshipped most frequently, was violence. When they weren't committing violent acts—brawling in the alehouse or beating their wives—violence seeped into their lives in other ways. It inflected their language. They often spoke of wounding and punishing, even killing. They wore their strength proudly, thumping fists on tables and slapping each other on the back.

If violence was their god, then the alehouse was their church; they congregated there most evenings. Robin didn't particularly like it, but he went every so often to show that he was one of them. If he never went at all, the men became suspicious. They watched him with mistrustful eyes.

Here they all were now, crowded into the low-ceilinged Swan. Robin had been fretting about his ferry ride with Pete Darling earlier; Pete seemed to have been testing him, and he felt as though he had failed. He wanted to curl up among the hens and be alone but decided instead to go to the alehouse, to renounce the gentleness he knew Pete sniffed on him like a scent.

He left his brother and mother by the hearth, and his father—who suffered sometimes from an aching head—lying in bed, and made his way alone. Once or twice he turned to say something to Dickie, but Dickie was not with him; it was a surprise each time. As soon as he was through the door of the alehouse, he saw that he'd made a mistake in coming. John Shirly, standing on a stool, was announcing with a grin that he had a treat in store for them all—words which touched Robin's skin like frost. A treat for drinking men could only mean one thing: something was going to be hurt that evening. Something might even be killed.

The air hummed with excitement. Some of the men had brought dogs, which growled and yelped at their feet. People spilled ale onto the floor, their cheeks reddening, sweat gathering on their brows. Temperance was serving drinks at the bar. Robin liked her and was glad when she had time to talk; he saw something familiar in her face, a false hardness he shared. Sometimes, she groaned aloud at the sight of the assembled men and raised her eyes as if to heaven, and it cheered him to think that someone among this loud-voiced throng was akin to him. But today she was too busy even to look at him, and he found himself alone.

"Here, Wildgoose," Pete Darling said, staggering over, "have a drink."

He took the cup and drank quickly and deeply, as a man might drink. It looked as if Pete had been drinking all day; his eyes were red as crab-apples. It amazed Robin that Pete's drunkenness never seemed to hinder his ferrying. He could drink enough to fill a coursing river and still guide the ferry across the water without any trouble, balancing on the wide wooden deck as though he were completely sober.

Through a gap in the heaving crowd, Robin saw that John Shirly had disappeared. A shriek sounded outside. "Hear that, lad?" Pete said, smacking him on the back. "It's time for the baiting."

Robin gasped: ale had shot up his nose when Pete hit him. The men exchanged smirks and began to pack towards the door, stepping out into the gloaming light, and Robin trailed behind them to join the circle that had formed in the yard. The shriek sounded again—a heart-chilling noise—and he saw that it came from a rocking barrel inside the ring, something scratching agitatedly within it. Pete was beside him; glancing over, Robin found that a lustful look had settled on his face. His flaming eyes were quick and busy, but his other features had grown sluggish. His mouth stretched into a lazy smile.

John Shirly upturned the barrel with a stick, and the baying began. Lads took up stones to throw. One man stepped forward with his dog, a drooling mastiff. "Go on, boy," he said, in a low, smothered voice, as though his whole life depended on it.

The dog seemed to smile, following his nose to the opening of the barrel. Robin couldn't see the creature—a badger, most likely—but watched the faces of the crowd beyond, seeing their eyes widen. He heard the intake of breath, a squeal, and saw the dog retreat with a bloodied nose. Its owner hung his head in shame.

Another dog was brought forward, and another, terriers, bulldogs, and mongrels. People wrestled and shoved, pressing closer for a better look. The ground was now spattered with bright pools of blood, and the men were growing restless. No one had been able to draw the badger out. It was a matter of pride that the badger be killed, a matter of manliness; the creature couldn't be allowed to live. One man—brave, or perhaps merely drunk—staggered forward and brought his fists down heavily on the barrel. Someone else lurched towards it and kicked into the opening. Now, several of the wounded dogs returned, and together they dragged the badger into view.

It was smaller than he thought it would be, with brilliant white flashes on its face and little black eyes. A chunk had been taken out of one of its ears, and there was blood across its back. It stayed low to the ground, alert. Out of nowhere, one of the dogs took it by its neck and shook it from side to side. Some of the men started to cheer. Robin wondered if he was going to be sick.

He closed his eyes, and when he opened them again he saw that it was over. The badger fell as if dead, and a shout arose from the crowd. Men began pressing forward to administer kicks.

"Go on," Pete said, pushing Robin by the shoulder.

He didn't want to kick the badger. He looked up and found Temperance watching him with an expression which seemed to him too much like pity; an expression like that could unmask him at any moment. He stepped forward, swallowing, to the mound of black and bloodied fur and joined the general kicking. He was very near to tears.

But now—Robin struggled back, afraid—the badger was on its feet again and lashing out with pointed teeth and scratching claws, and a woman somewhere screamed, and the circle drew back. The dogs were no match for it; even the men carrying sticks and cudgels couldn't contain it. Robin saw it darting around the circle and willed it to escape, but it was impossible—there was nowhere for it to go. The man with the mastiff urged the dog to set on it again, and he saw the dog pounce. He heard a shriek like the sound of a girl being murdered; it left a ghost-note in his ears, haunting him. The mastiff shook the badger until it was dead, then dropped it in a thin heap on the ground. Some of the men cheered and stamped their feet, but most stared in a mute daze, as though this wasn't the triumph they had hoped for. The badger had made a mockery of them.

After a while, they left the blood-stained yard and trooped back into the alehouse, where the drinking continued. Robin set down his cup, determined to leave. He didn't like the mood in the room. Despite the death, the men's lust hadn't been satisfied. He could see it in their eyes: they wanted more.

He left the alehouse and exhaled heavily. He hated it there—he always hated it—but to stay at home seemed to invite trouble. He consoled himself with the thought that he wouldn't have to go back now, not for a while. The men had seen him; for the time being, they would be mollified. When he didn't show his face at the alehouse, preferring the warmth of his mother's hearth, that was when trouble started. He had known it before—the muttering, the accusing looks.

It was dusk, but Robin could make out in the dwindling light a man lying by the door of the Swan, and a few others staggering back to Greater Nettlebed. He picked his way down to the riverbank, where he found Pete Darling—Pete always seemed to know when people needed to cross. He paused, recalling Pete's drunkenness, then took a deep breath and stepped onto the ferry without a word. The evening air was very still.

"Wily creature, wasn't she?" Pete said, punting them over the black water.

"The badger?" Robin said.

"Yes. Wanted her liberty, didn't she? Quite touching, in a way."

Robin looked up at Pete. He heard something scornful in his voice, something that told Robin he would have killed that badger a hundred times over if he could.

"Just a bit of fun though, isn't it," Robin said. It was not how he felt—it was far from how he felt—but it sounded like something a man would say. For some reason, in that moment it seemed especially important to sound like a man.

Pete glanced at him, and he saw in his face a look of suspicion which made Robin's stomach turn. He was silent, willing the ferry across the water. At last, they reached the far bank. "Thank you, Pete," he said, his voice a croak.

He stepped onto the grass but was held back by Pete's hand on his arm. "Where are you off to now, lad? Got a sweetheart somewhere, have you?"

Robin looked at Pete's hand: the width of it, the callused fingers. "No," he said. "I'm going home."

He wriggled free and walked with purpose along the road. He listened, but no footsteps followed. Night was descending rapidly now, and he didn't at first notice the pair of figures on the road ahead of him. Twin shadows, barely discernible in the thickening twilight. It was only when he was level with them that he saw who they were: two of the Mansfield sisters, their arms linked through each other's, their heads lowered.

They gave him a startled look, then laughed. "Oh, Robin. It's only you," one of them—Elizabeth—said.

The other, Anne, gave him a smile. "We were walking and lost track of time. It's past cockshut now, we should be home."

The offer came to his lips: he would walk them back. He liked the girls, and they didn't live far from his own cottage. He wouldn't want Master Mansfield to worry. But something stopped him from saying the words. He swallowed them and nodded mutely. Perhaps he had been infected by the mood in the alehouse that evening. Perhaps it had worked its way into his body, tainting his thoughts and instructing his tongue.

"You shouldn't be out this late," he said.

"Robin!" Elizabeth said, slowing to a halt.

"You ought to be more careful, miss. This isn't a good time of day for girls to be roaming the roads."

He placed a special scornful emphasis on *girls*, the way other men did.

"Robin," Elizabeth said again. There was a question in her voice.

The smile faded from Anne's face. She looked at him expressionlessly, then began walking on, pulling Elizabeth with her.

He watched them go. A sick feeling spread from his stomach to his throat as they disappeared into the cloaking darkness. It wasn't right, what he'd done. He'd been playing, pretending, but the girls didn't know that, and now they were walking home alone. He wished he hadn't let them go. He wished he hadn't kicked the badger.

The feeling grew large and ungovernable. It seemed to Robin that something terrible had happened, or was just about to. This was no ordinary feeling. It felt—he couldn't describe it—like a whistle, or a thunderclap, or a noose. He tried to push it away. He was just tired, he told himself. That was all. Everything would be fine in the morning.

He walked up the lane towards his home. He got quite far—past the old oak tree and the sun-bleached rock that Dickie particularly liked. He was almost at his cottage when he stopped. His heartbeat rang in his ears, and his fingers played restlessly with the hem of his shirt. The girls—maybe he should go back and check on them. Yes, he would go to the farm and make sure they'd arrived home. He broke into a run then—why, he didn't know. The road had been empty. The girls would be all right. And yet—

A noise reached him through the night air. He slowed, then stopped, trying to understand what he was hearing. It sounded like barking. Of all the words in Robin's reach, barking came the closest to it. It was deep and hacking, a cough that became a howl. It frightened him. He loved dogs deeply, even wild ones, even biting ones, but this sound unsettled him. This was no dog. It was a person barking, a person deranged into believing themself a dog.

He took a step towards the noise. The road had been empty, apart from the two Mansfield sisters. This disturbing sound, could it be coming from—

He took another step. The blood was pumping so loudly in his ears that he could hardly hear the barking now. Perhaps he was imagining it. Or maybe it really was a dog. Yes, he thought, clutching a fistful of long grass, crushing it between his fingers. It was probably just a dog, maddened by the fight with the badger. He choked out a laugh. That was it—the badger. It had put fear into the village's dogs. That's why this dog was behaving oddly, gibbering like a demon.

He dropped the grass. The barking continued, roaring in his ears, tormenting him. He couldn't ignore it; his conscience forbade him. He needed to see what it was.

Thoughts plaited themselves across his restless mind, the same thoughts over and over. He wished he hadn't left the girls. He hurried back down the lane, dread burrowing into his body. He wished he hadn't kicked the badger.

By the time he made it to the road, the barking had stopped, and there was no sign of life. He stood and stared, wondering what to do next. After a while, he thought he saw someone emerging from the gloom, but he didn't step forward to meet them. Instead, without thinking, he ducked deep into the bushes. He held his breath as the figure approached, twigs forcing into his clothes and hair.

It was Pete Darling. Robin felt himself freeze. Pete Darling—heading back down to the river, where Robin had left him no more than half an hour earlier. He had come from up the road where the girls had been walking, but Robin didn't want to connect the two things. He wanted to exist in murkiness, in the uncertain summer dusk. In that moment, certainty appalled him; he would hate to know where Pete had been or what he had done. He closed his eyes as Pete passed, praying that he wouldn't be seen. His body was ringing, and the sick feeling grew greater. At last, Pete disappeared. Silence descended on the road and the dark hedgerows. Robin stepped out, shaking, and ran up the lane to his home.

SEVEN

SOMETIMES, JOSEPH LIKED TO LIE DOWN IN THE ORCHARD and listen. It was harder now, with his knees; he risked never getting up again. But when he was down there, touched by the soft grass beneath his body and the dappled sunlight on his skin, he felt as though a great weight was lifted from him. He listened to the bees humming through the wildflowers and the birdsong overhead. He smelled the ground's fresh, earthy smell. Catchrat might pad over and fold herself into the crook of his arm, and Joseph would doze and dream.

That day, a particularly warm one, he walked from the stable-yard to the well and reached with bony hands for the rope, pulling up a bucket from which to wash his face. The water was cold on his skin, a delicious shock. Refreshed, he ambled towards the orchard and felt for a cushioned patch onto which to lower himself. It was late afternoon, but the sun still shone hotly. The orchard was thick with the flavours of high summer, fruit and herbs and flowers at their finest.

He closed his eyes and listened. There was mewing nearby; Catchrat's kittens were playing in the grass. A bird rustled in the apple tree above him. Beyond, he heard the weathervane being nudged a creaking inch by the breeze. He breathed out.

He liked to lie here, not least because it took some of his fear of death from him. This fear needled him late at night; it made him feel as he had sometimes felt as a boy, struck by terror while the world was sleeping, wretched and alone. He knew it was approaching—it had taken his son and daughter-in-law, and now it had come for his wife. He was next, he saw it up ahead; the question of what it would be like tormented him. He didn't believe in the vicar's nonsense, in hellfire or heaven, but he envied his certainty. What lay before Joseph was unknowable, a gape. It scared him. Yet lying here, on this summer afternoon, he soothed himself with a question: How bad could it be to be buried in the warm earth and listen to the world conduct itself around you? That didn't seem so dreadful. He breathed in deeply. No, not so dreadful. For a moment, the simmering fear subsided.

He had waves like this, waves of worry, that approached—lapping, threatening—then receded. Sometimes they were about death; often they were about his granddaughters. About their fortunes, their security, the money that seemed to come and abruptly go. There was always something to worry about. He tried to picture a worryless life, but his mind couldn't summon it. He breathed out, listening to the bees.

At the far end of the orchard, he heard the sighing of skirts moving through long grass. He tried to guess which of the girls they belonged to. He heard heavy footsteps and a whipping sound, a stick beating against nettles, and knew it was Hester. The second girl was more difficult, slighter and silent, but he judged from her pace and the careful way she seemed to be lifting her dress away from the ground that it must be Grace. He didn't alert them to the fact that he was lying there—perhaps he should have done. He dozed and listened to the girls, their voices mingling with the sounds of the bees and the complaining weathervane.

"Hester," Grace said, very quietly. "What's happening?"

The whipping paused. "I don't know."

"Can't we make it stop?" Grace whispered.

"No." The stick was struck once more against the grass. "We can't."

"Why?"

"We just can't. We don't have the power."

"But . . ." A hiccough. "Tell me, Hester—please. What actually happened to them?"

Hester's voice was rough. "I'm not sure. Something . . ."

Joseph frowned.

"Was it in the village?" Grace asked.

He struggled up, propping himself on his elbows. "Girls?" he said, straining to see them. "Is everything all right?"

He thought he heard something—a stick being stuck into someone's side. "Everything's fine, Grandfather," Hester said. "Sorry to disturb you. We didn't see you there."

"You didn't disturb me," he said, pushing himself to his feet. He stood, panting: it got more difficult each time. "What are you two talking about?"

They were silent. Then Grace said, "Nothing."

He raised his eyebrows. "Nothing?"

He heard rustling—Hester striding towards him. "It's just a game we're playing, Grandfather. A bit of make-believe. The others are under attack—from pirates."

"Pirates?"

"Yes."

He looked at her. She was close enough now for him to see her dark hair and black dress, and the stick she held, thick and curving like elder-wood. He peered down at Grace. "Is this true, Grace?"

He couldn't see her expression. "Yes," she said.

"I thought Elizabeth wasn't taking part in your games any more, Hester. Ever since you bruised her arm during Blind Man's Buff."

Hester scoffed. "That wasn't my fault. She was taunting me." She paused; he could see her admiring her stick. "Anyway, she's forgiven me now."

They were silent once more. Joseph let his shoulders drop; he couldn't make them speak. "Go along then, girls. And be careful, won't you?"

"We will, Grandfather," they murmured, brushing past him.

He lingered, but the orchard had lost its charm. The waves of worry were rising again; he needed to keep busy, to distract himself. He walked back to the house. Inside, he was struck by the smell of roses. "What's all this?" he called.

He followed the fragrance to the hall. Reaching towards the table, he touched piles of silken flowers, mountains of them.

"Careful, Grandfather," Elizabeth said from across the table. "You'll prick yourself."

He looked up but couldn't make out her face. The roses formed a pink and yellow blur, soft, stretching. "What are you doing, child?"

"I'm making rose water for your eyes."

He heard in her voice something guarded.

"But this must have taken you all day—"

"I wanted to do it."

He could hear her tearing the petals from each stem. They came off with a gasp.

"What about the pirates?"

"What pirates?" she said.

"The pirates . . . Hester told me you were all playing some game."

He heard her sigh. "I don't play games with Hester any more."

"I know, I—"

He felt almost heady from the sea of roses. He stepped towards the table. "Is everything all right, my dear?"

The plucking continued, the fragrance growing stronger. "Yes, Grandfather," she said quietly.

"Where's Anne?"

"She's resting."

"That girl works too hard. You all do."

Elizabeth said nothing. More petals were torn. Dizziness descended.

"I'll go," he said. "I'll leave you. Thank you for doing this, my child."

"It's my pleasure," she said. He thought he heard her voice crack.

"If there's anything you need from me," he said, "anything at all, I'll be in the parlour."

He listened, but she didn't move. He left, bewildered.

These girls—sometimes he didn't understand them. They told him one thing when they meant another. They turned themselves inwards. They were contrary, they confused him. The previous evening, for instance, Anne and Elizabeth had arrived home late from their walk. Joseph spoke to them quite firmly. He hardly ever told them off, but he had spent the preceding hour watching darkness fall, worried. He needed them to know the risks. He couldn't see their faces, but he imagined them laughing at him. They usually did, teasing, mocking his concern. Funny, though—he hadn't heard any laughter last night. They'd crept upstairs, unspeaking.

And now Elizabeth, who didn't like housework and usually had to be coaxed to do it, had picked every rose in the garden. Perhaps she was trying to make amends for their late return home last night, or maybe she merely wanted to be busy. Joseph would never know; he couldn't ask her outright. He only hoped the girls would talk to him if they needed to. He didn't like to accept—though the thought occasionally occurred to him—that he might be the last person they would turn to. They had a whole household of sisters to confide in.

He made his way into the parlour to escape the clinging smell. Sitting in his chair, he tallied the girls in his mind. Anne was resting. Elizabeth was making rose water. Hester and Grace were conspiring about something. Mary, the littlest, was often found trailing behind one of the others—but where was she now?

He pushed himself back to his feet, exhausted. "Mary?" he bellowed.

"Yes, Grandfather?" a small voice said from behind his chair.

"Goodness! You startled me, child."

"Sorry, I thought you heard me. I'm being a cat."

He sat back down. "Very good. What kind of cat?"

"A black one. A witch's cat."

"Very well, my love."

She pawed at his hand, which was dangling, listless. He frowned. "Is everything quite well with your sisters, Mary?"

"I have no sisters. I'm an only kitten."

He nodded. "The girls who live here, then. Do you think they're quite well?"

She stopped toying with his sleeve. He heard her become still.

"Mary?"

He fluttered his fingers, as though enticing a cat. She pounced and rubbed her nose against them.

"Mary?" he said again, more gently.

"Well," she said. "I heard from Catchrat that some of the girls have been behaving strangely today."

Joseph frowned. "Strangely? How so?"

"All sad and sullen. Not stopping for cats."

"All of them?"

She gave a small meow. "It started with the older two. But then the middle two started acting odd too."

"And the youngest one?"

She screeched. "There is no youngest girl. There's only me, and I'm a cat."

"Sorry. Yes, of course."

He was silent for a moment. "What do you think it is, Mary? Is it their grandmother?"

"It isn't their grandmother."

"Is it me, then? I fear I was too firm with Anne and Elizabeth last night."

"No," she said. "You're never too firm. You don't know how to be."

He fluttered his fingers again. "What, then?"

"I don't know." Her voice was a whine. "They won't tell me."

"But if they do tell you, will you tell me, Mary? I'm getting quite worried."

She huffed. "For the last time, I'm not Mary. And no, I won't tell you."

"Why not?" He felt aggrieved.

"Because that's tattling."

"What if it's nothing? Then you can put this old man's mind at ease."

"It's not nothing."

She was no longer a cat. She sounded unnaturally serious; he was startled by her tone. "What is it then, child? Please—you're alarming me."

"It's . . . not nothing," she said again.

He heard her pick herself up. "I'm going to find one of the others now," she said. "They're better at pretending than you are."

He listened to her ascend the stairs to their bedrooms. *Not nothing*. He turned the words over in his mind. Not nothing could be anything. Not nothing was formless and vast. *Not nothing*, he thought. *Not nothing*. He repeated it to himself until the words became empty. *Not nothing, not nothing.* Like the lapping of waves, he brooded. *Not nothing*—like a quick-rising tide.

EIGHT

WHEN THOMAS WAS A BOY OF TEN OR ELEVEN, WITH scraped knees and dirt under his nails, his mother had taken him to Oxford to throw stones at grown men. Hunger had embedded itself into his family by then. It found its way into their bones; it froze them. There were days when he and his brothers stewed dandelion leaves for soup, tricking themselves into fullness with bowls of bitter green water. They planned how their fortunes might be made. Thomas's youngest brother would set out in search of a city made entirely of gold. His middle brother would court a noblewoman and accept from her gifts of garnet rubies and glowing pearls. And Thomas, laughing weakly at the lengths he would go to impress the pair, told them how he might murder someone for money. Yes—lying on the ground between their thin bodies, feeling the wind whistle in beneath the door: he believed himself almost capable of it then.

He believed himself capable again in Oxford that warm May day. He and his mother joined the hustling swarm of other women, other hungry boys, who had gone to the market to accost the bakers and millers, pleading with them to lower the prices of corn and flour. Thomas saw in the men's big, whiskered faces an ugly look, the idea of profit. He had good aim and sent dusty stones in their direction. He remembered the feeling, the sound of pebbles hitting cotton, calfskin, hair.

He thought about that day now and then; it reminded him that manhood had begun a long time ago. Recently he thought about it for other reasons. Would he have thrown stones at Joseph Mansfield, who had, by all accounts, done so well in those years of scarcity? What about the sisters—could he have stoned them too? What did it mean that he could live here among them, could grow strong from meals of mutton and pies and wheels of cheese made with their own hands? What did it mean that he didn't dislike them?

It was the girls. The way the girls lived, the way they spoke and laughed and worked, was a source of endless fascination for Thomas. They were like a rich tapestry, he thought, beautiful to look at but more interesting, more rewarding, on closer observation. He saw how the threads interwove, how one complemented the rest. He saw alliances form and then draw apart. He saw how they braided together, how they were at their strongest when all five threads pulled around each other.

At meals he was silent, listening to the sisters talk. He heard how Grace had found Catchrat with a bird in her mouth; its wings hung all oddly, she told the others over dinner. She nursed it in a wooden box in the parlour, carrying beetles and worms in cupped hands from the garden for its meals. He heard how Hester had developed a new passion for barbering; with scissors stolen from Elizabeth's work basket she had snipped sections of Mary's hair into upright tufts. He heard Elizabeth, twisting a little gold ring round her finger (their mother's, Grace later told him), speak longingly of going to

London, or even Oxford—Oxford would do—to see the ladies in their fine attire. He heard Anne talking to her grandfather about the farm and the house, about the money she required for weekly produce at the market.

His eye became more discerning. He saw that clothes which belonged to one or another of them floated around the family, like weeds carried along on a current. A pretty, lace-edged cap would appear first on Anne's head, and then a few days later on Elizabeth's. One of Hester's dresses might get torn and would be passed on, patched, to uncomplaining Grace. He saw how Hester and Mary sought mischief together, how they teased Elizabeth for her vanity and doted on Grace. Anne was loved by all in the burning but inattentive way that children love their mothers.

When he closed his eyes, he saw them. Elizabeth's arched eyebrows, Mary's missing teeth, the spread of freckles over Hester's nose, the bitten edges of Grace's nails. And Anne—it was Anne's face he saw most often of all. It came upon him without warning: in the final moments before falling asleep, working in the yard, washing. It haunted him. The lines that formed on her forehead, deepening when she listened. The downward slope of her mouth, her small white teeth. Her wide blue eyes, which—when they rested on him for too long—brought the colour to his face and neck and made him turn away. He had been wrong when he thought she wasn't attractive. It was as though he had first seen her face at night and found it obscured somehow. As the days passed, something changed. She became different, illuminated: dawn had arrived. He realised he had been mistaken before; he had missed something extraordinary in her. Now it was brilliant morning, and he saw her more clearly than ever. He understood that she was beautiful.

He was unable to be natural around her. They often encountered each other during the day—he helped her carry things from the farm to the kitchen, or built fires for her, or accepted dumbly as she passed him plates of food. Some days she barely seemed to see him; on others she observed him with a directness that spoke of disdain. Both were hell—Thomas was surprised to discover how keenly he felt it.

He was like a man diseased. It infected him swiftly and absolutely; he had no resistance. One day he was himself, someone with little interest in girls, who preferred fighting with his brothers or drinking at the alehouse. The next he was somebody entirely different, transformed into a person whose sole interest seemed to be in her.

He searched for clues about what she thought of him, as a pig searches for food in mud. He listened closely to Connie's chatter, hoping she might let slip something she'd overheard Anne say. Late at night, he scoured the day's interactions with her, looking for some sign that she returned his secret passion. There was none; she seemed entirely unaffected by him. He dug further, he foraged. That inhalation yesterday when he walked past her—maybe that meant something? The dark rings beneath her eyes; perhaps he could claim those too. He hated himself for these thoughts. They demeaned him. And yet, he decided with complete sincerity, he felt he might die without them. The idea that she could be suffering a sleepless night because of him was keeping Thomas alive.

At last, desperate, he decided that he would test her. He would break her guard down somehow to find out what she was feeling. Perhaps she saw in his face an earnestness that allowed her to be complacent. He would become distant. He would extract from her some sign. His restless mental foraging could be concluded at last.

Haymaking had not yet started, but Joseph, lifting his nose in the garden, told Thomas it would soon—he seemed able to smell the far-off grasses starting to set seed. In the meantime, the cherries wanted picking. Thomas followed the girls into the dappled orchard, the air rich with the scent of ripening fruit, a wicker basket clutched to his chest. Clusters of cherries hung from bowing branches, sunlight glistening on their wine-dark skin. Hester let out a whoop, and Grace gave a nervous giggle. Thomas's heart rose; he felt he too could laugh or shout. He saw Hester pull a branch roughly towards her, and the cherries rolled onto the grass by her feet.

He found a tree within sight of Anne and began filling his basket. Mary followed him, watching.

"Do cherries grow where you come from?" she asked with a frown.

He looked down at her, amused. "Of course, Miss Mary. I come from Milton, not the moon."

She digested this. "I wonder if there are cherries on the moon," she said eventually.

He paused, pretending to consider. "I should have thought so," he said. "Otherwise what do the moon people eat?"

"The moon people!" Mary said. She frowned harder; this was a novel concept, one that would require further thought.

"Yes," Thomas said, smiling, "don't you know about them? They're very tall, and very pale, and once a month, when there's no moon at all and they have nowhere to live, they come down to earth for a night of mischief and revelry."

Mary's eyes widened. She observed him with suspicion. "How do you know all this?"

Thomas looked around conspiratorially. "Don't tell anyone,"

he said in a low voice, "but I'm actually a moon person myself. Just here on a little visit. Someday soon I'll go back home."

He gestured to the sky with an upturned thumb.

She appeared to be biting the insides of both cheeks. He saw her appraising his golden hair and found a flicker of delighted discovery in her face, which she quickly concealed.

"And your family," she said, "your brothers—they're all moon people too?"

He paused. "Yes," he said. "They are. They're still on the moon though."

"Oh," she said. She glanced at him. "You must be lonely without them."

"Sometimes," he said. "Wouldn't you be lonely without your sisters?"

She nodded. "I don't know what I'd do without them. I'd want to get back to the moon as soon as possible, if I were you."

He grinned to conceal an unexpected painfulness in his chest, brought on by her pitying look. "Let me get back to picking cherries," he said. "I've got to do as much work as I can before I leave for . . . you know where."

Mary nodded solemnly and walked off to mull this information over further. Through burdened branches, Thomas caught sight of Anne. She had been listening, it seemed, and was smiling at him. Her face, when she smiled, became softer. The hardness around her mouth melted. He resisted the bone-deep urge to return her grin, to walk over to her, to laugh together, and went back to his work. He realised he had been holding his breath and allowed himself to exhale slowly. When he reached up to pick the cherries, he found that his fingers were trembling. He plucked one and rubbed his thumb over the skin. Her face: there had been something unusual about it. It was configured differently today. The rings beneath her eyes were darker, and her skin was paler. Was she ill?

Oh, how he hated himself then. He was a bully. He had ignored Anne when she was ill, and he wouldn't forgive himself for it. Cherries were thrown into his basket urgently, forcefully. He took great fistfuls from the tree and tore. He would pick every cherry in the orchard, and then he would hurl himself into the river to meet the wretched end that he deserved. She had smiled at him even though she was ill, and he had cold-heartedly ignored her. How could he be so—

He heard shrieks beside him. Mary, her face smeared with cherry juice, was whispering into Hester's ear, and Hester laughed with unguarded delight, her eyes on Thomas. She too had blood-red stains down her chin; her open mouth was filled with the pulp. She grinned at him appreciatively.

He continued with his work, feeling the heat of the climbing sun on the back of his neck. Hester and Mary had now given up all pretence of picking and were chasing each other through the trees, their hair falling around their faces. Grace worked quietly on the far side of the orchard; her basket brimmed with heaped cherries. Thomas looked over at Anne and found that she had left her place. Elizabeth was absent too. He picked up his basket and moved through the orchard until they came into sight. The dark outlines of their dresses appeared through heavy branches; they were standing close together.

Mary and Hester had disappeared into the kitchen garden. The orchard was quiet now, except for the occasional sound of cherries tossed against wicker. Thomas stopped his work and listened, his hand outstretched so that he could resume his task if somebody saw him.

Elizabeth was crying. He knew it was Elizabeth because Anne never cried, and because everything Elizabeth did, even blowing her nose in a square of linen, she did prettily; the sobs that reached Thomas rose and fell like lovely music. Anne's arm was cast around Elizabeth's shoulders; she cradled her closely but said nothing, staring at her feet. Watching, Thomas wondered why Anne didn't try to console her sister. This wasn't like Elizabeth's usual little upsets, her fits of pique, soothed by promises to go to Oxford or to the fair. This time, she seemed aggrieved by something massive, something lost. It was the kind of grief for which there was no consolation, and Thomas saw in Anne's face that it burdened her too.

Girls shouldn't feel sorrow like this—that was Thomas's first thought. This was the sort of sorrow to be found on the faces of the very old, people who'd seen many deaths, suffered years of hard winters. The sisters looked, he thought, as if something had been stolen from them.

Thomas watched. His body was uncomfortable in its clothes, his undershirt scratching his skin. The sun felt heavy on his head. He wanted to sprint, to swim. Instead, he stayed very still, observing the girls. He saw how Anne continued to do nothing, frowning, her arm crooked tightly around Elizabeth. Two spots of pink stood out on her pale cheeks.

At last, Thomas saw Anne lift her hand to her sister's face. "Do you trust me, Lizzie?"

She hiccoughed and nodded.

"Good. I promise all will be well. Do you believe me?"

She nodded again.

"Very good. Come, let's try and forget about it. Have some cherries—they're your favourite."

Thomas watched through the leaves as they ate. Elizabeth

grew calmer, her sobbing soothed. She ate delicately, nibbling, wiping the stain from her lips with her pocket square. But it wasn't Elizabeth he was watching; his eyes barely strayed from Anne's face. Anne's mouth. She tore through the skin of the cherries with pointed teeth. She ate as an untamed animal eats, biting, chewing, the juice bleeding around her lips and down her chin. He was beguiled by her abandon. He wanted to watch her eat forever.

Observing the ravenous way she devoured the fruit, Thomas discovered a kind of hunger in her that he had not known before. The look on her face was one of wildness. He saw strength there, and ferocity, and merciless resolve. It thrilled him and made him ill at ease.

That evening, unsleeping, he would return to the scene and try to make sense of what he saw. (Maybe the girls were mourning their grandmother, he thought. But why such fresh pain? No—it must be something else. Sickness, perhaps. Or matters of the heart.) But that was later. In the cherry orchard, he could do nothing but watch. He didn't work, or think; he merely watched. Unplucked cherries clustered around him, but he couldn't bring himself to care. Even when Anne looked straight across at him and saw him staring, he didn't mind. He was sure she had seen in his face his naked longing, but there was nothing he could do; he was transfixed by the sight of her. He would have done anything in that moment. He would have knelt at her feet right then and there, would have killed for her, would have died for her, even. Yes, he realised with some bemusement—he would do whatever she asked. She had bewitched him completely.

NINE

Temperance hadn't seen the Mansfield sisters for several days when they walked past her on the road, all five in a row. She smiled at them—to be friendly, and because she pitied them in a way—but only one of them returned her smile. Grace, the second youngest. The others stared back blankly. They strode with purpose, turning down the dusty path to the river.

Walking back along the road, Temperance saw the impression they had made on the village. The old women hunched over their pillow lace, sitting in their doorways to catch the last of the day's fading light, folded up their work and went inside. Playing children stopped to watch the girls pass, their laughter stifled. A muttering, mangy dog fell silent.

They looked particularly severe today. It wasn't merely their clothes, which were still black; something rankled in their faces too. Temperance eyed their expressions, uncertain what she saw there. It seemed as though they were angry with everything: the sound of the birds, the air on their skin. Even Mary, the littlest, looked harder somehow, her usual milk-toothed grin replaced with a cold glare.

She found Pete on the riverbank, idly measuring the height

of the water on his pole. "Lower than last year," he said when he saw her.

"It'll be dried up before long," she said, shaking her head.

"And then what will I do?" he said. "I'll have a new wife to look after; I can't afford for people to just walk straight across."

She clucked sympathetically and stepped onto his ferry. He pushed off, still frowning.

"Your wedding will be on us soon," she said. "Just over a fortnight to go."

"Yes," he said, staring at the water.

"Have you made your cottage nice for your bride?"

He shifted his frown to her face. Temperance shook her head. "Doesn't matter. She'll be very happy, I'm sure."

Her voice warbled a little, as it always did when she lied. She knew things about Agnes Bullock, Pete's betrothed: how she went to church doused in perfumed waters so strong that Temperance, several pews back, had been overcome by the sickly scent; how she had a collection of lace-edged handkerchiefs which she never used but took out routinely to stroke and admire; how her father adored her and her mother did not; how she believed herself to be in love with Pete Darling, whom her mother had placed in her way at church one day; how she had never seen his ramshackle cottage; how her love might not withstand the sight of it. Temperance was quick and curious; she remembered every word ever uttered in the Swan. There were scholars at the university in Oxford who knew all manner of things about the earth and the heavens, and she believed herself akin to them. Her field was humbler but no less complex: she was an authority on the inhabitants of Little Nettlebed.

She looked out. At dusk, the river was deep green and glassy.

All along the bank, clusters of figwort, just beginning to bloom, were doubled in the dark water. A corncrake's grating two-note call carried on the evening air. "The Mansfield girls are going for a walk," Temperance said. "Funny time of day to do it."

Pete looked up. "Which girls?"

"All of them, even the youngest. All five walking along the river."

She squinted at the path to see if she could see them. The light was becoming thinner. She found this time of day deceiving—it didn't have the honesty of the morning or the bright afternoon. At this time, nearing cockshut, things were not always as they seemed. Colours changed, and shapes shifted. Dim light deluded the eyes.

"Those girls . . ." Pete began, before falling silent, allowing the gentle rise and push of the pole to fill the air.

"What about them?"

"There's something . . . unholy about them."

Temperance felt a tingling at the back of her neck. "Nonsense," she said swiftly. "They're just a little wayward, that's all. They have no parents. The old man doesn't know how to discipline them."

Pete grimaced. "No," he said. "No, it's more than that. The other night . . ."

He stopped, and she turned to look at him. His expression was wretched; she hadn't seen him like this before. "What other night?"

"No," he said again. "It doesn't matter. There's something wicked in those girls though, I can tell you. I've seen it with my own eyes."

She crossed her arms. "What have you seen?"

He looked at her, then over at the far side, searching for the sisters. "Unholy things," he said at last as the ferry met the bank with a bump.

She stepped onto the shore. "Nonsense," she said again, this time with less conviction.

He said nothing. It was clear he wasn't paying attention. The corncrake sounded into the silence, harsh and unearthly. "Good evening, Pete," she said eventually, and began making her way up the path.

"There they are now," Pete said, but she wasn't sure if he meant for her to hear; his voice was low.

She turned and saw them, barely discernible on the far side of the river. They were picking their way around tussocks of wildflowers, mignonette and sweet-smelling agrimony, their outlines seeming to merge and draw apart like moving shadows or pools of ink. Their faces alone stood out from the dark bank.

Yes, they troubled her. They left her with a cold feeling. She pressed up the path, towards the road and the alehouse; she wanted to be inside, where there was candlelight and a bright, hot fire. The murky dusk made her uneasy. As she reached the gate at the edge of the meadow, she heard a noise. At first, she thought it was somebody shouting, but it was too deep, too wordless, for shouting. It sounded more like—

"Temperance," Pete cried, and she hurried back down the path, uncertain what she would find there.

She came to him, disturbed by his staring eyes and lily-white skin. "Temperance," he said again, a whisper.

"What, Pete? What was that shouting?"

Shouting, she said, because she was too afraid to say the other word: *barking*.

"The girls," he said, his eyes searching the far bank.

"Temperance, I swear . . . I saw those Mansfield sisters. I saw them turn."

Her hammering heart suddenly quietened. "Turn?"

"I swear it," he said again. "I was looking at them across the water, walking along the path. Five of them there were, five walking figures. And then, like *that*, they began to change. Growing close to the ground. Running on all fours. Barking."

She could do nothing but repeat his final word. "Barking?"

"They were dogs," Pete said. "Those girls turned into dogs before my eyes. I swear it."

"You swear it?"

She looked at him and then questioningly across at the far bank. He swore it. But what did that really mean? Pete swore many things. Once he swore he'd seen an angel step onto his ferry; she and John had laughed about that for a long time afterwards. When he was a boy, the body of an otter was found in the rushes by the river, its neck wrung like a chicken's. Pete swore he hadn't killed it. It had been a dog, he said. A devilish big dog. But one of the farmhands had seen him, and later he confessed with tears streaming down his face. He didn't know why he'd done it. Which was all to say: he had sworn before, and his swearing hadn't amounted to much.

The problem, this time, was that she almost believed him. There *was* something strange about those girls; Temperance had seen it herself. She could just picture them, shifting, changing, their feet becoming large and padded, rosebud mouths extending into snarling jaws. She shivered.

"Pete," she said, looking at him. He turned his thin face to hers; his eyes were bloodshot and wild. "Promise me you won't tell anyone about this. Not a soul."

"Why shouldn't I?" he said indignantly.

"Because you don't know what you saw, not really. Listen to yourself—five girls turning into dogs! I've never heard such nonsense. You were mistaken." She gestured to the quick-settling night. "It's dark. You don't know what you saw."

He pouted like a child deprived of a treat. "People should know. The villagers—they might be in danger."

"Hush! No one's in danger. The only danger is in you spreading unfounded rumours."

He scowled at the river.

"Pete? Promise me. Otherwise I shall be forced to tell John we can't serve you any more. Too much ale addling your brain."

His face acquired a look which she had only seen once or twice before—an expression of outrage and revulsion, generally reserved for women who tried to tell him what to do. Temperance folded her arms, disturbed. Eventually he nodded and spat.

"Good," she said. "Thank you."

She looked around. The gate was barely visible now. "See you tomorrow," she said, following her feet up the path, keeping the quiet river behind her.

The alehouse wasn't full; a few men were playing cards here and there in candlelit alcoves. They looked up when she entered but didn't seem bothered by her breathlessness or her discomfited air. She tried to calm herself.

"What kept you?" John asked as she approached the bar. "Just popping out to pick up some bread, you said."

She lifted her basket. "I've brought the bread. I was waylaid at the ferry, that's all."

She looked up at him. His face gave her comfort: those large pink cheeks and laughing eyes. "I was talking to Pete."

He bent down to pick up a pile of firewood. "Oh?" he said, but she could see he wasn't really listening. He walked across to the large open fire and stoked it violently. She saw the sparks leap across the hearth.

She stood beside him and watched as he threw a log onto the embers, as the smoke mushroomed around it and the fire took hold. She found curious patterns in the licking flames—figures, faces. People warping into creatures. She looked away.

"Pete was talking nonsense at the river," she said.

John had his arms crossed beside her, watching the fire, as she was.

"Another one of his stories, was it?"

"Yes," she said. "I fear this one's a bit more . . . dangerous."

"Dangerous?" John looked down at her.

"It's about the Mansfield sisters. He says he saw them turn into dogs."

She saw John's eyes widen.

"Nonsense, of course," she continued.

"Seems a curious thing to claim," he said.

"Come now, John. You said it yourself. He makes up stories."

He nodded. "And drinks a fair bit."

"More, recently," she said. "He's been fretting about the river—losing work for the season if it all dries up."

"Maybe he's nervous too, about his wedding. It's an odd match, that one. Why her parents permitted it I don't know."

Temperance pursed her lips. "No one wants a spinster daughter. And anyhow, they claim to be in love."

"Yet they have so little in common."

"I'm sure they'll be very happy."

But she wasn't sure, and to disguise her uneasiness she

looked up brightly and tapped him on the chest. "Were you nervous when you got married, John Shirly?"

"Nervous?" he said, laughing. "Not a chance."

He pulled her towards him. She nestled into his front, breathing in the scent of his clothes, the wood smoke and the hops.

"I was over the moon," he murmured.

She looked up at him and smiled. This was when their marriage was at its best, when they remembered themselves in the first flush of love.

"Now, woman," he said, releasing her, "let's put aside this nonsense from Pete Darling. Make yourself useful and pour these fellows some drinks."

She nodded; she had a job to do. Slowly, she pulled on her hide gloves and moved towards the men, resolving to think no more about the Mansfield sisters.

TEN

Perhaps his future wife had changed since she'd accepted his offer of marriage, or perhaps, Pete conceded, he hadn't known her well enough to start with. Now, every time he visited, he discovered something new about her. These new discoveries weren't always to his liking. She was obsessed, it seemed, by beauty: in her face, in her clothes, in the gifts she liked to receive—but when he took her to the river at sunset one day, the sky ablaze with heavenly pinks and reds, she had merely been bored. Sometimes, when he spoke in the company of others, she would place a soft hand on his and say, "What Mister Darling means is . . ." followed invariably by something he didn't mean at all. It made him feel as though he were visiting from a foreign land, with Agnes his overzealous translator. Worse was when she talked about their "love" as though it existed outside of themselves. What was their love like, she would ask, and he would fumble for suggestions. Their love was like a river, he said, beautiful and strong. Their love was like a field in summer. A basket of plums. A dove. (Sometimes his answers seemed to satisfy her; at others, apparently at random, she would take offence. "A picnic?" she would say, her eyes filling with tears. "*A newly mended road?!*")

Spending time with Agnes was not always a joy, but it had never occurred to Pete not to marry her. He tried to visit her at least once a week because it seemed to please her; he considered it a duty, and the fulfilment of duties made him feel agreeably pious. The more onerous the duty, the closer it brought him to God.

That morning, with only a fortnight to go until they were wed, he approached her father's house with a posy of freshly picked wildflowers in his hand. Buttercups, cornflowers, and honey-scented camomile—he pressed them to his face and breathed deeply. They gladdened him, summoning to mind the meadows along the river. He hoped that she would like them, but a quiet voice inside him told him she might not. He was quickly learning that the things which brought him joy so often did the opposite for his future wife. She longed for porcelain and embroidery and other fine gifts. Looking at the quick-wilting stems, he found them lacking, weed-like. He dropped them to the ground and felt sorry.

The maid took him through to the parlour, and there he awaited Agnes, despite knowing full well that she had seen him from the window. This was a little dance she liked to do, and Pete obliged her, adding it wearily to the list of things he'd never understand about her.

"There you are, my betrothed," she said, entering. "How nice of you to visit."

He shrank from the word *betrothed*. He didn't know why, but it made him picture long, throttling tentacles.

"I came to see how you are," he said, bowing slightly. "Not long now until our wedding."

Her butter-yellow hair fell in tight ringlets around her face, in the style of a younger woman. When she laughed, her ringlets shook. They were shaking now.

"Everything's in order," she said. "Let's hope the weather stays fine."

He frowned. The weather, day after rainless day searing the dry ground, was far from fine. They looked at each other for a moment, and Agnes smiled brightly. They were still feeling their way into intimacy, despite the period of their betrothal. On her breast she'd pinned the brooch he had given her when the betrothal was confirmed, a golden fish, its face carved into a delicate gasp. She played with it sometimes, rubbing her thumb over its scales. He didn't like it when she did this; he worried that she was wearing it down. The brooch had been his mother's. It had been difficult to part with.

"With the wedding so soon, perhaps one day we should visit your home and decide what we no longer need," she said. "We'll be wanting new things, of course."

She beamed at him, but he didn't smile back. He saw her close her mouth and felt cruel; she was unhappy with the size of her front teeth, he knew. He stepped towards her and took her hands in his, clearing his throat. "Of course," he said. "Whatever pleases you, my dear."

Her ringlets shook. She was appeased.

"Have you been into the village recently?" he asked, withdrawing his hands.

"No," she said, moving towards the window. "Any news?"

He looked at her. Should he tell? He knew her fondness for chatter. Disclosing a secret to Agnes was like casting a lit taper into a hayrick.

"I do know something . . . Something very strange. About the Mansfield sisters, it is."

She looked up quickly. She shared with her parents a keen interest in the doings of the Mansfields. Her father viewed Joseph Mansfield with professional envy; her mother didn't like the size of his house. Agnes was jealous of the closeness the sisters shared, their tight, inward-looking circle. Her own two sisters were married and mean.

"Strange?" she said. "What do you mean?"

He fumbled for the words to describe to Agnes what he had seen. Her world was not his world. She lived in a separate, simple place. Angels never alighted there; girls never turned into dogs. He would have to think carefully about how to describe this to her, how to make her see.

"Those girls," he began, "they played a trick on me."

She had been standing, but now she sank into a chair, her eyes fixed on Pete's face. Pete sat down opposite her.

"A trick?" she said faintly.

"Yes," he said. "I don't know how it was done, but they tricked me. I saw them walking along the path yesterday evening, just as the light was fading. All five of them, it was. Even the littlest. They were walking as normal, and then—I don't know—I saw them . . . I saw them become something else."

"What was it they became?"

"Dogs," he said.

"Heavens," she said, her hand on her mouth.

"Yes," he agreed.

"But how did they manage it? The trick? Did they hide in the bushes and release the dogs?"

"Maybe," he said, folding his arms. "I don't know how the trick was done. But they knew I was watching. I believe they wanted to scare me."

Agnes raised her eyebrows. "Why should they want to scare you?"

He gave her an ugly smile. "They're wilful girls. They need no reason."

She observed him for a moment. "Perhaps it was just a bit of fun," she said. "A game."

He shook his head. He saw now that he had gone about this the wrong way. "It wasn't like that—a game, a bit of fun. Devilry was at work, I know it. When I say they became dogs, I don't mean they hid themselves and released five dogs. I mean I saw their bodies change. I saw them grow fur and teeth. I saw tails emerge from their petticoats."

She leaned towards him, her eyes round. "No," she said.

"What do you mean, no? It's true."

"I must tell my father." She fiddled with her sleeve. "But are you quite sure of it—of what you saw?"

Pete didn't like this. "Of course I'm sure," he said, standing, agitated. "What are you suggesting—that I'm making it up? That I'm mad?"

It occurred to Pete that he did sound a little mad, raving here in Humphrey Bullock's parlour. That was the problem with unearthly things, things sent from heaven or from hell: they made witnesses seem like madmen.

"Of course not," she said, reaching for his arm, pulling him back down to his seat. "But you must admit this is all a little odd. I wouldn't like my father to think you're easily tricked."

He bridled at this. No one could trick Pete Darling. She was growing supercilious; she believed she knew better than him. He asked himself then why he had committed to marrying this woman. He had thought her submissive but was beginning to realise that the only person she really submitted to was her father. Yes, she brought with her a little wealth from her father's trade, but Pete could live comfortably without it. The reason this betrothal had come about at all was that he'd thought it his duty to get married, just as Adam had married Eve. In Little Nettlebed there weren't many Eves to choose from. He first spoke to Agnes at church one Sunday when her mother dropped her handkerchief in his path, but he hadn't considered her a possible bride until he saw her in Eden one night in a dream. (It was true that—like Eve—she'd been naked in the dream, but that wasn't the point; the dream was an instruction from God.) He reminded himself of this now. He had received God's instruction. He was meant to marry Agnes Bullock.

He swallowed. "I'm sure I'm not mistaken."

She stood up. "Well, this is *very* peculiar. I'll tell Father—he always knows what to do."

He stood up too; he towered over her. "I'll call again soon."

"That would be nice," she said.

She tiptoed to place an inelegant kiss on his cheek. The kiss elicited nothing from him: no feelings of love or excitement, not even of uncleanness. He remembered the heat he had felt on his hand after helping Anne Mansfield from the ferry, the way it had lingered like a burn. He nodded at Agnes and left.

Walking home, Pete wondered if he had done right in telling her. John and Temperance Shirly told each other everything, and he admired that about them; it wasn't good to conceal things in a marriage. Yes, he thought, passing the church—he had only done the honest thing.

Down the road he loped, past barefoot children, their feet ringed with dust, and aimless chickens and panting dogs. A boy and an enormous pig ambled by, its legs unsteady beneath its broad, hairy weight; the lad absently tapped its tail with a stick. Women were carrying baskets of dirty clothes to the river. It was washing day, which meant—for the poorer women, the ones without wells—lugging their laundry to the Thames. Pete liked it when they gathered to do their washing; he would laze on his punt, listening to their chatter. He liked the way they plunged their clothes into the green water, the linens ballooning and sagging below. He liked how they pulled them up and wrung them tightly, drying tough hands on dirty aprons. He liked watching them work, seeing them bend into the river.

Today, though, they looked unhappy. The river was lower than it had been the week before, and the women were having to bend further. Some of the older ones could hardly reach, stopped by stiffened backs. He saw one of them—a young one, pretty—throw her husband's undershirt on the ground in frustration; a moment later, she picked it up and dusted it down meekly. Pete marched past them. These women had no right to complain. What were unwashed clothes to a man whose livelihood depended on the water? They knew nothing of frustration, of suffering. He was the only one who knew.

The pretty one came towards him with her basket of clothes ready for hanging. He saw her face arrange itself into a smirk. Even the tired, labouring women were laughing at him. Something about her expression made him think of Anne Mansfield—it was on this stretch of the bank that he'd seen the girls turn. He knew then that he had done the right thing in telling Agnes what had happened. The Mansfield sisters had meant to scare him. They were mocking him, testing him. In return, they would feel the full, scalding weight of his anger.

ELEVEN

As Pete foresaw, the story spread like quick-licking flames. By the time Robin came to hear of it—buying bread from Martha Heathcote—it had travelled all over the village and beyond. People were seized by it, entranced—so entranced that they didn't notice when the story started to change. Pete Darling thought he saw something at dusk; that was how it began. But the story soon shifted and grew. Pete was not alone in seeing something; a few villagers had witnessed it. Come to think of it, there had been several occasions when people had found something unusual in the girls. Sharp teeth—yes, they'd always had sharper-than-normal teeth. And dark hair. And glowing eyes, like the eyes of hungry dogs.

Not everyone believed what they heard. Some of the villagers recalled Pete's flaws, his old fondness for untruths. Perhaps some of them had been slighted by him in the past. Others felt him capable of scheming for his own ends. But even these people, the ones who urged caution as the story spread, looked within their hearts and found there a dark mistrust of the Mansfields. They were not normal, those girls. The story confirmed for everybody what they had always known: there was something unnatural about the five sisters.

As for Robin, the rumours didn't disconcert him. Short as his life had been, and confined as it was to the county of Oxfordshire, he was well acquainted with the many eccentricities the world had to offer. He had met people who lost great sums of money and regained it in miraculous windfalls. He had heard of ghosts and hauntings. He knew of a pair of ravens who nested on the roofs of those about to die. A tale of girls turning into dogs—that barely made him blink. What bothered him was the ugly, excited way Martha Heathcote recounted the story. There was something irresistible in it, like sweet cakes or marchpane; he could see her getting heady from it. He feared the villagers' appetite for oddness. It was clear to him that, true or not, the story was going to stick.

He liked the Mansfield sisters. At haymaking time, when he helped old Joseph Mansfield each year in the fields, the girls had only ever been nice to him, bringing him food and ale, sitting alongside him as he ate. Sometimes they surprised him: the jokes they made, the way they spoke about the world. They reminded him of boys with their little spars, their unabashed speech. He would be sorry if this story harmed them. It was sure to harm them somehow.

When Martha Heathcote told him, he made a show of indifference. He didn't like the way she watched him, grinning, fishing for a response. He felt, as he always did with village gossip, that the gossiper not only gave but took; something was required of the listener. Martha wanted him to exclaim, to show disbelief. She wanted the satisfaction of having surprised him. Instead, he looked blankly at his shoes. When she'd finished, he took his bread and left.

He hoped there would be a way to avoid the story, but it had seeped through the parish like sewage, filling every rut and crevice. He saw people leaning over walls to speak to one another, huddled in corners, heading to the alehouse. Their faces all shared the same look, the look of triumphant, disgusted discovery.

On the way back to his cottage, he saw Connie and Amie, the two maids from the Mansfields' farm; they walked quickly along the lane ahead of him. "How do you do?" he called to them. They too were often kind to him during haymaking—he got on well with Amie, the gentle one, especially. Her face, decorated with pockmarks from girlhood, made him think of a beautiful statue that had been weathered for years by wind and rain.

They didn't turn, and he called again. "Sorry, Robin," Amie said at last, her eyes averted. "We must get back to prepare dinner."

Connie looked around. "We can't dawdle."

"Of course," Robin said.

Perhaps his concern was written too plainly on his face. "I suppose you've heard the nonsense that people have been spreading about the Mansfield sisters," Connie said, frowning at him.

He fell in step beside them. "Well, yes. Nonsense, as you say."

"Dangerous nonsense. Girls have been called witches for less—and killed for it, even in my lifetime."

He felt something cool on the back of his neck, a breath. "Not any longer though."

"Perhaps not. But people still believe in the devil. The devil is as real to people as you or me—as that loaf of bread."

He clutched his bread uncomfortably. "You don't believe all that though, do you? The devil and all."

She scoffed. "Of course not. I'm not some country simpleton. I don't believe in magic either. Or wise women, or none of it. What I do believe in is sickness and plague." She gestured to Amie's face. "We've seen our share of sickness and plague, and I don't intend to suffer any more of it. If there's something amiss at the farm, if those girls are sick, we'll be leaving without a second thought, let me tell you."

Robin looked at Amie, whose cheeks were pinkening. Maybe she didn't like her face to represent sickness. Maybe she hoped her face would merely represent itself.

"Have you seen any sign that the girls are sick?"

Connie paused. Amie shook her head. "No sign at all," she said. "The girls are fine. Tired, maybe. They work hard. They're still grieving their grandmother."

They fell silent for a while. "It was Pete Darling who started the story, you know," Robin said.

The girls looked at him. "You think he wants to harm the Mansfields?" Connie asked in a low voice.

He felt his heart beat faster. He recalled the night after the badger baiting, when he'd seen Anne and Elizabeth, and Pete stalking off into the darkness. He remembered the barking he'd heard. "Perhaps," he said. Flour gathered stickily on his palms as he gripped the bread. "Perhaps not. I don't know."

Connie paused. "We'd best hurry, Amie," she said.

Amie nodded at him, and they pressed on, heads lowered. Robin trudged up the path to his cottage; it was quiet, lined with yellow ragwort and nettles. He slowed his pace, watching the bees and cabbage whites touch lightly on the flowers. There was not a breath of wind that day. The path, usually pitted with deep puddles, was completely dry, the mud scorched into crusted ravines. It was here that he had heard the barking noises the other night, the sounds that had so disturbed him. They were tied, in his thoughts, with the story Martha Heathcote had told him. Pete Darling, the Mansfield sisters, the sound of barking—each piece appeared in his mind, spinning round and round until he felt quite ill. He could just hear it, the sound. Like barking, but full of human feeling; no dog had ever felt so much. The memory of it made him shudder.

But now he could hear something else. Real, this time. Not barking but shouting. Panicked, he ran up the final stretch of path to find his mother standing in front of their cottage. Her face—often pink from cooking or from the nip of winter frost—was a flaming red, and, like a flame, she danced and trembled. Around her lay several dead hens.

"What's happened here?"

She looked up at him, incensed. "Our hens—they're dead. All of them. Killed this morning, it looks like, just as Richard and I were inside."

She gestured to the plump, feathered bodies on the grass. Seeing them, Robin felt a pang. They were all there: the one with the speckled markings on its back, the one with the fancy white collar. He mourned their warmth.

"Might it have been a fox, Mother?"

She narrowed her eyes at the hens. "This was no fox. No fox was ever so brazen. Broad daylight, it was."

Robin felt something catch in his throat. He looked at his enraged mother and hoped she would not say it.

"Looks like a dog to me," she said.

He exhaled. "Plenty of dogs in the village that could have done it."

"Perhaps," she said. She looked at him. "Richard told me something he heard in the village. The Mansfield girls have been acting all unusual, he said. Like dogs, he said."

Robin tried to spit. "Nonsense. You know it's nonsense, Mother. Dickie's still a child—he'll believe anything he hears."

"What if one day he hears the truth? Then he'll be right to believe it."

He shook his head. "Today is not that day."

Something passed over his mother's face—it pleased her when he wasn't weak. Her tone became conciliatory.

"We'll tell your father when he comes home. We'll see what he says about the matter."

"There's nothing he or any of us can do. There's no proof."

"Here," she said, pointing again at the dead hens. "Here's the proof."

He said no more, stepping inside with the bread. Richard was by the hearth, stoking the fire. He was shorter than Robin but growing urgently every day; he was on the cusp of manhood.

"Good day, Dickie," Robin said. "I hear you've been gadding about in the village."

He set down the bread, by now no longer yielding and warm but hardened after the hot walk home. Richard stopped stoking but didn't turn, and Robin eyed his brother's back, damp curls clinging to his neck. It was impossible, brothering a boy who wanted so much to be a man. Not just any man—a brave man, a strong one, who commanded the respect of other men. Perhaps this should have gladdened Robin, who had after all spent much of his life pretending to be such a man. But he dreaded the loss of his brother; he couldn't bear to give him up to the drinkers and the brawlers, the Pete Darlings of the world. And he would hate for Richard to cease thinking of him as someone worthy, his shining older sibling. He could see the change happening already—right now, before him, in fact. In the way Richard, facing him, didn't meet his eye. The embarrassed clenching of his fists.

Robin swallowed. He would be gentle and compassionate, as he always was with Richard. His beloved brother hadn't vanished yet.

"Now, Dickie, what did we talk about before? You mustn't repeat idle gossip."

Richard lowered his head, scowling.

"But Robin," he said, kicking the edge of the chair, his eyes on the floor. "Tubb told me. He swore it. Why would a schoolmaster lie?"

Robin frowned. Tubb had no business spreading this story.

"Schoolmasters are merely men, Dickie," he said. "Sometimes they tell untruths."

"But Robin," Richard said again, flickering a quick look at his brother before returning his gaze to the floor, "how am I meant to know when a schoolmaster tells an untruth? Especially when he swears it's true."

This, Robin conceded, was a difficulty. He thought for a moment. "In future, when something strikes you as curious, you should tell me first," he said. "I'll sift for you the true from the untrue."

He waited to see how this would be received. There was a time when Richard would have crowed with delight at such a suggestion—a shared task, Robin's treasured attention—but now there came a pause. Richard fidgeted with the idea before breaking at last into a smile.

"I'll tell you something true," he said, gathering close to Robin's side. He'd often done this as a younger boy—crowding him, his breath hot on Robin's cheek. "And this time I know it's true, for I saw it with my own eyes."

"Oh, yes?" Robin said, pleased. He sat down in the chair by the fire. The room was dim and warm; he felt sleep calling. "What did you see?"

"I was down by the river—it's such a fine day, and I thought I'd go for a walk—when what should I see, panting on the beach?"

Robin was awake again. He felt suddenly very alert. He looked at Richard. "What was it?"

Richard smiled, excited. He crouched down beside Robin's chair. "A loach, I believe it was. All stranded there in the mud. Still alive though. Loaches are as happy on land as in the water."

"Why was it stranded?"

"The water shrank. It's down to the farthest bulrushes now."

Robin leaned back in the chair. He had too much on his mind to think of shrinking rivers and land-living loaches. "It's awfully hot for the time of year, isn't it, Dickie?" he said, dreamily.

Richard beamed at him—relieved, perhaps, that equilibrium had been restored; glad not to have disappointed his brother in some unuttered way. "It is," he said.

TWELVE

Of all the deaths Temperance had seen—and she'd seen many—the ones in childbirth were the hardest. It had happened to friends of hers, happy and fat with new life. Sometimes the infant survived, but sometimes nothing remained, mother and baby both lost. Bearing children was a deadly act.

No expectant woman was safe from it, not peasants or fishwives or queens. Today, another beautifully sunny day, was the turn of the blacksmith's wife, a young woman whom Temperance had seen sometimes at church. She had heard the woman to be sweet-natured and gentle. Thank God, everyone said, the baby was fine.

Temperance left the alehouse to see the coffin being borne to the churchyard. John told her she was morbid, that she shouldn't trouble herself so much with death. It would come for her one day, as it came for everyone; there was no use fretting about it beforehand. And it was true, death did trouble her, but it was not for the dead she went to see the funeral procession—it was for the living. It was for the six pregnant girls whom they made carry the coffin, a warning of their possible fate.

This had been a tradition in the village for as long as Temperance could remember. No one knew how it had come about, and no one had ever seriously tried to stop it; the oldest and cruellest traditions were usually the hardest to cast off. And so, with each death in childbirth, the dead woman's coffin was carried by other women on their way to becoming mothers. It was a hard thing to witness, but Temperance felt it to be her duty. By some twist of fate or misfortune, she didn't seem able to bear a child. She would never face the fear these women had to face. The least she could do was to stand beside them, to show that she was with them in this ghastly hour.

She waited for a little while on the high road, watching for the procession. The sun burned above. Ants scuttled around her feet, seeking the cool green verge. The river was lower today, drawing into itself; it had taken Pete Darling only a few swift punts to carry her across. She hadn't raised with him his story about the Mansfield girls, which she had now heard several times around the village. It angered her that he had spread it, despite his promise that he would not. Perhaps he knew that she was displeased with him; he offered to accompany her to the procession and buy her a bun afterwards. She shook her head. This was not a time for buns.

There was no sound, but a change in the air told her that the coffin was approaching. Villagers gathered at their doorways and on the road, removing their caps and bowing their heads. Children pressed into their mothers' skirts. The coffin wasn't large, but the six pregnant pallbearers seemed to struggle beneath it. One woman at the back looked almost due, her belly full and heavy, her swollen feet shuffling. The face of the girl at the front was wet with tears; in the silent street her snatched breath was the only sound.

One day, Temperance resolved, she would speak to the

vicar about this tradition, but she knew already what he would say. Remember that death is everywhere: that was his line. To help himself remember, the vicar had furnished his home with yellowing skulls and dark, ugly oil paintings of skeletons and hourglasses. He would leave fresh flowers in arrangements around the house for weeks on end, until they wilted and crisped. Temperance tended to avoid visits to the vicarage.

The women trudged past. She tried to catch their eyes, but they looked straight ahead or down at the ground. She saw how heavily they breathed, how much they required rest. One woman in the middle, her pregnancy barely showing, looked greenish in colour. Dry mud dusted their feet and the hems of their dresses.

After they had moved on, people went inside their cottages or continued on their way. Temperance didn't follow; she had no desire to attend the burial. She tarried at the side of the road, not yet wanting to return to the alehouse and the men who required her there. For a moment, she wanted nothing but to think quietly about these women, and the many other women like them, and those unlike them too. She thought about what they all went through each day: the great, gruelling trial of being a woman in a world governed by men. How painful it was, and how humiliating. To be forced to hold your dead friend aloft because it was thought that you, in your smallness and stupidity, might not realise that this could be your fate. It made her tense and pale with rage.

She turned, not really knowing where she was going, and brushed against one of the Mansfield sisters. Anne. Temperance had a curious idea that Anne knew what she had been thinking; she found in her face a suggestion of sympathy.

Behind her stood the other four girls, still in their mourning clothes. Of course, Temperance thought. It was no surprise that they were here; their mother had died in childbirth when Mary was delivered. Perhaps, like her, they wanted to bear witness.

"Good day," she said and nodded her head.

They each returned her nod, but none of them spoke. She paused for a moment, searching their faces. Their expressions seemed veiled; even the youngest looked subdued somehow. She wondered if they had heard Pete Darling's tale. She wanted to find a way to ask them how they were, but she was distracted by a group of passing boys. One or two of them she knew, but they looked changed, here, among this group. They seemed bigger and harder, muttering behind their hands and laughing. "Beware of the dogs!" one of them whispered loudly to another, while a third made a sound like barking.

"Begone with you," Temperance said, chivvying them with her hands, but the boys only smirked.

She looked at the sisters, who watched the boys, unmoved. Quick, like a grass snake's darting tongue, Hester bared her teeth at them; they pushed away then, startled. Temperance turned back to the girls, but now Hester's snarl had disappeared and they were smiling at her guilelessly. Walking away, her heart felt heavy. How could she warn them that they needed to be careful? The world was more dangerous than they knew.

Preoccupied and keen to keep out of the alehouse for a while longer, Temperance ambled up the road towards the church. The bell was tolling, but the sound was ignored by the people who had gathered moments before to watch the coffin pass. Children ran along the road, women lugged great baskets of washing, someone was herding a line of geese with a stick.

Death was too frequent a visitor in Little Nettlebed; it couldn't keep their attention long.

At the edge of the churchyard, Temperance watched. She wasn't sure why she was there, but she stood behind the dark yew bushes and waited. The dead girl had been buried, fresh dirt heaped on her coffin. The mourners were dispersing. Temperance saw the vicar walking towards her.

"Good day, Vicar," she called—why, she didn't know.

He stopped and looked at her vaguely. She often realised this afresh, that the vicar's features—his wrinkles, his moles, the velvet patch tied across his head—were so familiar to her, yet she meant nothing at all to him. She was merely a nameless face in his congregation.

"I'm Temperance Shirly. My husband's John Shirly, the publican."

"Ah, yes. Good day, Temperance."

He made as though to walk on, but again she felt compelled to speak. "May I talk to you about something, Vicar? A sensitive matter."

He considered her more closely. Up and down went his eyes, over her face and body. "Of course. Would you care to accompany me on my way?"

She nodded and walked beside him. Where should she begin? There was a lot she wished to discuss with him, a lot she hoped to ask. She wanted to talk to him about heaven and hell and Jesus and the saints. And the poor pregnant pallbearers, and the souls of the dead. And the rain that never seemed to come, and her drunken father, and the hole in the vicar's head, and the story about the Mansfield sisters, and more, much more. Now seemed to be the moment for Temperance to share everything she'd ever wondered, all her curious thoughts and concerns; it was not often she had the vicar's ear.

He walked ahead of her, his long black robes caressing the daisies that lined the path. Temperance knew her audience with him would be brief. There was only time for one thing. The sisters—she needed to speak with him about the sisters.

"It's the Mansfield girls, sir, the granddaughters of old Joseph Mansfield, down at the farm."

"I see," the vicar said, not slowing.

"A story has been spreading around the village. I fear it could be very dangerous for the girls if something isn't done."

"Oh?"

The vicar, Temperance felt, believed village matters to be beneath him.

"I was hoping that you could help stop the story from spreading further. Perhaps you could speak to the man who started it, the rumour. Pete Darling, it was—the ferryman. Perhaps you could talk to him about the importance of speaking the truth." She trotted to keep up with him. "Pete has been known to make up stories before."

He slowed slightly, and Temperance saw his enormous brow wrinkle. "What is the story that Pete Darling has been spreading?"

Temperance cleared her throat. "It's about the Mansfield sisters, as I say. He claims"—she leaned heavily on the word, inviting the vicar to share her scepticism—"he claims that he saw the sisters turning into dogs. At dusk, it was; the light was very poor. I was with him that evening, and I saw nothing of the sort. He is . . ." She stopped short of the word *liar*. "A storyteller. He always has been."

The vicar paused. He observed her silently for a while, and she in turn observed the velvet patch on his head; she had never seen it so close.

"Before I talk to Pete Darling, I think I should speak with the girls."

She shook her head. "Please . . . If you don't mind me saying, Vicar, but I don't think there's any cause for you to trouble them. Their grandmother's not long in the ground, as you know. They don't deserve all this simply because Pete has made up a story about them."

He continued to look at her, unspeaking. She felt herself shrink.

"Please," she said again. "This is not what I meant by coming to you. The story is nonsense. Those girls need privacy, they need quiet; they don't need to be troubled by this business."

His eyes were very small, and his voice became small too, as though someone had constricted his throat. "In matters of the inner life," he said, "of privacy and quiet, I think we can wager that I have more authority than you."

She nodded, chastened, and the vicar walked on. He didn't invite her to follow. "Thank you for bringing this to my attention," he called. "I believe these girls need the help of our Lord."

Temperance said nothing. She watched him walk away. A ringing sounded in her ears as she made her way from the churchyard down to the river. At the river's edge, she stared at the naked rushes and reeds, exposed by the lowering water, and she thought about the Mansfields. She thought about their story as though it were a tale being told at the Swan—she had heard such stories, leavened with ale, so often before. Usually, Temperance knew, there came a moment in the drunken teller's tale when the story took a sudden turn for the worse.

Slam went the teller's tankard down on the table, and the pink-faced listeners gasped; there was no going back. This was that moment, she felt, as she summoned Pete to ferry her across. She had told the vicar something she shouldn't have, and now there was no going back.

THIRTEEN

THE AIR WAS HEAVY WITH HEAT. THE *LACK* THAT JOSEPH Mansfield smelled each morning had spread like a desert, swallowing everything around it. Gone was the scent of his beloved roses, the sweet honeysuckle and dew. Instead, he found only earth and withered grasses. He found basins of parched puddles. He found cherries rotted to the stone. A shroud of dust seemed to have settled on the garden. The moisture was robbed from his very mouth, his voice reduced to a croak.

It worried him. Their well was almost empty. Grace and Mary dropped stones into it every day to measure the depth, listening for when they hit the water; they had reached a record low. The other girls responded to the heat in different ways. Elizabeth lay in the garden in Joseph's own wide-brimmed straw hat, her long hair loose and wild. Even Anne, usually so neat and particular, had taken to padding around without shoes on; the stone floor was cool on her feet, she said. Unruliness had claimed Hester completely. Unbeknownst to Joseph, she had taken the girls' silver baptism spoons out of their case, angling them in the midday sun to test which would best set alight the crisping leaves in the orchard. The girls rarely reported on each other, but Elizabeth eventually told—fire, after all, was no laughing matter. Joseph followed the smell of singed leaves to its source and dragged Hester and the five spoons back into the house. She gleefully recited her findings as they went: her own spoon was, of course, the finest fire-starter, followed by that of Anne, then Mary, then Elizabeth, and finally Grace.

Meanwhile, the river was thinning, baring its banks, the lilies and figwort shrivelling in the heat. Already, their vegetables were dwindling, leaves whitening and wasting, despite the fabric canopies Grace fashioned above them. The quinces and crab-apples they sold as jelly would rot and fail, and haymaking would be dangerously hot—they were due to start that week. A bad summer meant a hard winter. A hard winter meant death for many.

"How has your sight been, Grandfather?"

Anne was applying the tincture to his eyes. He tried to draw his thoughts away from the worrying heat, towards Anne's voice. There, he heard something pinched and panicked.

"Not too bad, my child. Summer is the best season for me. Sometimes, in bright daylight, I can make out shapes quite clearly. I milked Fillpail yesterday without any trouble at all."

He waited. It was true—his vision improved in the strong summer light. In winter, the gloom never lifted; no amount of candles or fires could pierce the darkness. Recently, his sight seemed better than it had for a long time. His granddaughters' faces occasionally swam into focus, and he had sudden flashes of illumination: the flowers on the painted wall-hanging in the hall, the rosy underside of an apple, thick curls unseating Mildmay's cap.

"That's good," Anne said, but her voice had not lost its small, vexed quality; there was a tremble at its edges.

He turned his face towards her and said gently, "How are you this morning, Anne?"

Perhaps he could make out her dark eyebrows, drawn closely together, her thin, downturned mouth, the proud thrust of her chin. Shapes drifted in and out of the fog. "I'm well, Grandfather. We're all well." She paused. "There's been some difficulty with Hester, but I'm sure things will improve soon."

"What sort of difficulty?"

She had been applying a linen to his face, but now her hands withdrew. "I'm sorry to trouble you with this, but Hester's flowers have arrived and she's taking it very badly. There's been a lot of crying and climbing of trees."

"Climbing of trees?"

"Yes."

"She wishes she was not a woman?"

"Yes, she says she'd rather be a boy. Or at least a woman who's allowed to live like a man, like Joan of Arc. Or failing that, a pebble."

"A pebble?"

"Yes. She says pebbles look very peaceful and are unencumbered by ugly things like blood and breasts."

"I see." He thought for a moment. "Should I speak with her?"

"I think you'd better not. She's not very pleased with the idea of men at the moment. She's already thrown a shoe at Thomas."

"I see," he said again. He smiled—he couldn't help himself. "She's a spirited one, isn't she?"

"Yes, Grandfather. Very."

His smile broadened. "Hester reminds me of your grandmother. She also had a spirited streak, you know."

"I remember."

"She didn't want to marry me at all. Did you know that?"

"I did, yes."

"She ran away! A week before the wedding. We found her halfway to London. Imagine what the village had to say about the matter."

"How did you persuade her to come back?"

"I told her simply that if we got married she could run away as much as she liked, so long as she left a message with someone telling me where she was going. But she never ran away again."

He folded his hands in his lap and beamed. "I always appreciated that about her. I liked the fact she knew her own mind." He softened. "I was proud to marry her."

He heard a sigh. The sound was new to Anne's alphabet; she wasn't prone to wistfulness. His gaze passed over the outline of her face. He cleared his throat.

"One day it will be your turn, Anne. To fall in love, to marry."

Her dress rustled; perhaps she was embarrassed. She did not, like Elizabeth, daydream about her future—the future made Anne uncomfortable. But there was something more. Her breathing had become quick and uneven. He felt her shoulders stiffen. A suspicion started forming in his mind, and when she tried to change the subject, he knew. His wife had told him to expect this day, and now—too soon, he felt—it had arrived. His eldest granddaughter was in love.

"This heat," she began.

He wished, as he had wished so often before, that he could see her face. He wanted to know what it looked like, Anne in the first flush of love. She was growing, changing, and he was being left behind. He wouldn't question her about it. He wouldn't even trouble himself with wondering who it was she'd fallen in love with. Some lad from the village, most likely—someone entirely unsuitable. It would end, as first loves always did, and she would marry a more fitting man. Occasionally, perhaps, over the course of her long and level life, she might sit and wonder at the fierceness of that first love, the mad unsuitability of it. Yes, Joseph saw it all. Anne was too sensible to let this ruin her. He would try not to worry.

"Indeed," he said, his face betraying his emotion. "The heat. And Hester." He swallowed. "If she doesn't settle, she might have to be disciplined. We can't have her climbing trees forever."

"I'll talk to her. I'm sure she'll be fine. It's just a bit of a shock, I think."

"Very good. Thank you, Anne."

At breakfast, they all pretended they couldn't hear Hester's crying carrying through the windows from the orchard. At last, Mary cracked and let out her own answering moan, low and heartfelt—she always did as Hester did. Joseph waited to see what the others would do; they were wildly unpredictable, as a rule. But today, good sense prevailed. "Please can you pass the porridge?" Grace said stiffly over the laments of her two sisters. Elizabeth started to giggle.

Joseph put a hand on Mary's shoulder. He knew how much she looked up to Hester, how alarming Hester's nameless affliction might seem to her. He sympathised with their tears, but his head was beginning to ache, and he was aware, at the end of the hall, of Connie's silent judgement. He didn't discipline the girls enough, he knew.

After breakfast, he found his way to the outhouse where the farm equipment was kept and felt for the cool, curved blades of the scythes. He planned to sharpen them ahead of the haymaking. He pulled one out, deliberate and slow, working the pumice carefully along the metal. It warmed beneath his hands. Work like this was pleasing to him; it lent his thoughts a rhythm. He thought about Hester and Anne, and how quickly the girls had grown, and what he would do without them when they were married and gone. He and his wife had brought them up as they had brought up their own son, with interests and dreams. Perhaps it had been a mistake, he thought, to let them believe they could reach beyond what the world expected of them. The world expected so little.

His hand slipped, and he felt the blade nick his skin. He heard running in the yard. It was Mildmay—he could tell by the boy's breathing. "Sir," Mildmay said. "It's the vicar. He's here to see the girls. I think you'd better come."

Joseph scowled, setting down the scythe. He had no interest in the vicar.

Outside, he found brightness. Sunlight seeped like warm water over his scalp, and his feet scuffed on the dry ground. He heard shouting, or crying, he wasn't sure which. A shadow hovered at the edge of the orchard. It approached.

"There you are, Farmer Mansfield."

"Good day, Vicar. To what do we owe this honour?"

The crying continued. It was Hester, sitting in an apple tree. He gestured for her to come down.

"Please come inside. It's hot today."

He couldn't see the vicar's face, but he heard in his voice something uneasy, almost fearful.

"I've come to talk to your granddaughters. About a very

sorry business—one which appears to be a lot more serious than I first supposed."

Joseph had been trying to guide the vicar to the house but turned when he spoke. "What's this about?"

"It's about the girls, Mansfield. I believe they are in danger."

Joseph gestured again at the tree where Hester was crying—violently this time, flapping his hand for her to go inside. The crying continued. "Danger?!" he said. "What nonsense."

"I'm perfectly serious. I believe the devil is trying to take possession of these girls." He lowered his voice with the air of someone at a party disclosing a scurrilous fact about his fellow guests. "You must have heard what people have been saying in the village."

Joseph hadn't heard—he didn't want to hear. But the vicar seemed intent on telling him.

"It's been going around that your granddaughters have been . . . Well, let's just say something extraordinary has happened to them. People are saying they've changed. That they turn at certain times of the day into dogs. That's what's being said."

Joseph expelled the air from his nostrils. "Don't be so ridiculous, sir. We live in an enlightened age. Stories of this sort belong in the past."

"Singular things will happen, whatever age we live in. Science cannot suppress mysteries."

The air was very hot. Joseph felt suddenly as though his legs might give way.

"I cannot indulge this. I'm afraid I must ask you to leave."

"But sir. Your granddaughters are in grave danger."

Joseph scoffed, but he felt his hands trembling. "They are

not. Look at them." He threw his hands around him, not knowing who was there. "They are girls. They are perfectly well."

"Why is one of them howling?"

"Howling? Not howling, crying. She is suffering. Her grandmother recently died."

He turned towards the sound. "Hester! Get down from there and stop that immediately."

The howling—*crying*—quietened a little.

"They are perfectly well," he said again.

"I wish you would let me speak with them, but I see your mind is made up. Still, I will see them on Sunday, and in the meantime, I will be praying for all of you."

"Very good," Joseph said. "Good day."

He waited, but the vicar's shadowy outline didn't move. "Vicar?"

He heard a sound like a fish gasping for air.

"Are you well, sir?"

"The girl . . . Something happened to her. There, beyond the trees."

There was an awestruck note in the vicar's voice. Joseph turned, exasperated. "Get inside at once, Hester!"

"Not the howling girl. Another one. She looked . . . She seemed . . . *changed*."

Joseph narrowed his eyes but saw nothing. "Who's there? Grace? Elizabeth?"

"She's gone now." The vicar's voice seemed very distant. "So strange."

"The heat is confusing you. I'll get one of the girls to bring you some water."

"No," he said. "There's no need. I'll be on my way."

Again, Joseph heard the curious, confounded tone. The vicar spoke slowly, dazedly. "Please," he said, "when you realise the peril those girls are in, bring them to me. I will try to help."

The vicar became a shadow which grew hazy and faded. Joseph breathed out and reached to find something with which to support himself. "Who's there?" he said.

He felt Mildmay's arm. "Here, sir. Lean on me."

He drew another breath. "Did you hear what the vicar said, boy?"

"I did, sir, yes."

The boy's clothes were moist with sweat. Joseph gripped his shoulder. "Did you see something? Just now—did you see what the vicar saw?"

He waited. The orchard was silent; he wasn't sure when Hester's howling had stopped.

"I saw something, very fleetingly. It looked like a trick of the light."

"What was it, boy? Speak!"

"It was Miss Anne. She was walking through the orchard, I think to bring Miss Hester back to the house. The way the dapples fell on her face, it looked like . . ."

Joseph's hand dug into the boy's shoulder. "What?"

"For a moment, through a curious trick of the shadows, it looked as though her face was changed."

"Changed?"

"Yes, sir. Into something else."

Joseph tried to gather himself. "Anne?" he called.

"She's gone inside with Miss Hester, sir."

Joseph shook his head. "This is very unfortunate. The vicar—he'll use this, I know. He'll scare people with it."

Mildmay faced him. "What can we do, sir?"

He sounded anxious, but beyond the anxiety lay something else. For the second time that day, Joseph heard the familiar strain. There was a suggestion in Mildmay's tone, something akin to love—the breathlessness, the fullness of feeling. He peered at Thomas. Was it love? Or was it something else—fear, perhaps? Maybe the lad was afraid. In that moment, Joseph was himself afraid. He squeezed Thomas's shoulder. "There isn't anything we can do. We must hope that nothing comes of it."

But Joseph was a farmer, and he knew what was likely to grow. The seed of this story would find fertile ground in the village. He dreaded to think how quickly it would flourish.

"We can't sit around all day dwelling on this nonsense," he said eventually. "I should get back to the scythes." A little task—preparing the scythes—might keep his mounting worry at bay. Joseph had learned this after the death of his wife: little tasks were the foot soldiers in the ongoing battle against despair.

He didn't ask for help, but Mildmay led him across the yard, and Joseph was glad. He felt old and tired, as though the interaction in the orchard had leeched the lifeblood out of him. Without the boy's support, he feared that he might fall.

Inside, he didn't immediately return to his work, resting instead on the bench by the door. Yes: he was tired. The tiredness claimed him completely. He wondered whether he should speak to Anne about what had taken place, trusting that his granddaughters were removed enough not to know what was afoot in the village. At length, he decided that he wouldn't—not until there was something more substantial to warn them about. Why trouble the girls with a rumour? And yet, despite deciding this, despite repeating to himself that it was merely a malicious story, a feeling of foreboding settled on Joseph and didn't lift for the rest of the day. He wished, for the first time in his life, that his granddaughters were different. Biddable, meek: the type of girls about whom rumours were never spread. He wished, for their sake, that they didn't invite strange stories.

He put his face in his hands. His wife would think him so weak.

FOURTEEN

All that was natural and good seemed to slip away from Thomas that night. Sleep never visited. It left him—raw-eyed, unrested—entombed in cool white moonlight. Words fled from his tongue. He could have sworn—. She had become—. It lay beyond language, what he had seen in the orchard. The next day he found he had no appetite for food. His arms would not lift. His legs would not walk. No one emerged from the house apart from Elizabeth, who crossed the yard softly first thing to fetch water from the well. Through the unlatched stable door, he saw her pass: hair undone, dreaming look. It was the first time he hadn't wanted to see any of the sisters; he shrank back into the scattered hay and the shadows and waited for her to return inside.

What was this place? Not just Mansfield's farm, although looking around now he felt queasy at the sight of the perishing beds and rotting fruit. Something about this village—the entire village—had infected him. His brothers would never believe it: that he, Thomas Mildmay, had made himself a slave to some affluent farmer's granddaughter, a sometimes-ugly girl, a girl who turned into—. He stopped. Little Nettlebed had made him forget. He had forgotten who he was and where he'd come from. He needed to remind himself.

There was still no sign of the old man, and anyway Mansfield rarely checked on Thomas's work. It would take him only a couple of hours to walk home; he could go and come back in a day. Or he might never come back—yes, he could free himself from this ungodly village for good. It comforted him to think it, although he knew in his soul that he might never be freed from Little Nettlebed. It had marked him forever: its people, its dreadful rumours, its difference.

And now his legs were moving. He was away—past the orchard and through the gate, not daring to look back at the house, not wanting to see any altered faces in its windows. The day was growing hot, but he didn't feel burdened by the sun on his back, or the sweat drawing serpentine designs across his skin. He was buoyed by the prospect of seeing his home. His mother, his two brothers, perhaps even his father when he came in from his labour. To see their snug cottage at the bottom of the dockleaf-studded lane—he could have danced with the dizzying joy of it. That was a place he knew and loved; it was where he belonged.

The sight of Pete Darling on the bank of the river stopped him short. The man was a vulture; Thomas saw it at once. The shape of Pete's crouched body, long neck extended, the hungry way he watched the water. He had a carrion-eating face. Still, Thomas consoled himself, this might be the last time he'd have to be ferried by Pete. He placed his coins into Pete's large hand and stepped onto the boat, facing the meadows on the far side, beyond which lay Greater Nettlebed and, many miles eastward, his home.

"Where are you off to then, lad?" Pete said behind him.

Thomas didn't move. "Across the river," he said simply. "I have business on the other side."

"Ah," Pete said.

A rasping sounded as the belly of the boat grazed the riverbed, and Pete fell silent. They passed the family of swans Thomas had seen on his first day here; the grey-downed cygnets had grown, their fluff replaced with slick brown feathers. One of them was missing. The church bell tolled in the distance, and the sound carried solemnly across the still water, unseating a gang of crows which lifted, cackling, from the ground. Turning towards them, Thomas found on Pete's face a terrible expression: he looked stricken, his skin suddenly pale. Pete caught his eye and grimaced. His pole slipped on the rock and he fumbled and nearly fell, righting himself at the last moment. The ferry swayed; Thomas held his breath until it steadied.

"Sorry, lad," Pete said at length. He sounded choked. "The church . . ." He paused. "I'm to be married in a week."

It felt unnatural—the ferryman almost falling into the water. Pete had always seemed so sturdy, as balanced on the river as he was on the bank. Thomas said nothing, and Pete cleared his throat, pushing hard on the pole.

"Someday you'll see, boy," he said, his voice gruff. "A man's wedding is a fearful thing."

For a moment, coming like a sun-filled crack in the clouds on a stormy day, Thomas allowed himself to imagine what it might be like to be wedded to Anne. For a brief, beautiful moment, there it was: a bride and church bells and everlasting bliss. He could have lived in this daydream forever.

When the ferry arrived at the far side, he stepped off and raised a hand in awkward parting. Pete's embarrassment had embarrassed him in turn; he didn't linger. Dust rose like smoke as he trudged up the path. On the road, earthworms writhed in the rutted cart tracks. The white plumes and watery blues of the Swan's hanging sign were dazzling today, but he wouldn't be drawn in. He was going home. The road to Greater Nettlebed glimmered in the morning sun.

He took a step, and another one, then slowed to a halt. The door of the alehouse opened, and Temperance emerged with a broom.

"Good day," she said, seeing him dithering in the road.

He inclined his head. "Good day, Mistress Shirly."

She had served him drinks before, but they hadn't ever spoken much. He'd seen her quirks—the way she flinched each time ale slipped over the rim of a tankard, her stiff leather gloves—but he liked her all the same. Her face was affable and inquisitive. She was short like his mother.

She started sweeping the step. "Going somewhere?" she said.

He looked along the road. "Just—." He gestured vaguely.

She narrowed her eyes. "There's no market today," she said, a question.

"No," he admitted, scuffing a line in the dirt with his foot.

She waited. "Listen," she said carefully. "Come inside, why don't you? Eat something before your journey."

She pushed open the door to the alehouse's dim interior; a sweet, almost stagnating smell carried on the air, the smell of yesterday's sweat and spilled ale. He cast a last look along the bright homebound road and followed her in, skirting around stools and wooden tables, his eyes adjusting to the low light. Smoke gathered like pooling incense in the rafters, and ash and scattered playing cards carpeted the uneven floor.

"Here, lad," she said, placing a plate of bread and cheese

before him. She pulled on her gloves. "I expect you'll be wanting a drink too."

Without the crush of warm bodies, the raised-voice roar, the Swan felt eerily empty, a skeleton robbed of its organs. Thomas frequented the alehouse every so often; he liked to drink and gamble, to be amongst other men. Sometimes he felt shaped by the girls—changed. After such a long spell in their company, three or four Sundays since arriving in Little Nettlebed, he needed time apart from them to remind himself who he was.

Temperance was watching him. "You know, I hear things here. Rumours and what-not. Whatever's said in the village—whether it's shouted on the high road or whispered behind closed doors—I soon come to hear about it. Drink unleashes even the most closely guarded secrets."

He looked at his plate and said nothing.

"Are you running away?" she said.

He shook his head. Perhaps he was, but he could never admit it: he liked to think of himself as someone who could withstand any threat. "There isn't anything to run away from," he said at length.

Temperance's face revealed nothing. She stooped to collect the fallen cards and busied herself with the broom, sweeping shards of sunbaked mud across the boards. Thomas took a sip of ale, lulled by the sound, the wordless company. Through the window, the church and distant cottages, the diminished river, were warped by the thick glass.

He ate silently, frowningly, wiping his mouth on the back of his hand when he'd finished. Continuing to sweep, Temperance said, "I had a man in here a couple of days ago. Wealthy once, though he lost everything in a fire last year. Everything."

She propped the broom against a table and put her hands on her hips, surveying her work. Thomas saw how some of her hair had loosened from its hold, wisping around her face, and a flush had seized her cheeks. "His house burned entirely to the ground," she continued. "A stray ember, it was."

She brought a clenched hand upwards and unfurled her fingers like flames.

"I'm telling you this because of what they found afterwards, after the fire burned and the water failed and the house was lost. There, among the scorched foundations, lay the ruins of another house. An ancient house. Roman," she said. "And there they found bits of crockery just like ours, and bracelets, and bones."

Thomas wondered what response she wanted from him. He tried to look interested.

"It was all exactly the same," she said with a smile. "All of it. The larder, the hall, the latrine. Nothing had changed in hundreds of years." She paused. "Nothing ever changes."

Thomas nodded. He saw what she was trying to say: that history was round, that all things pass. But she was wrong to think it about this situation. There had never been anyone like the Mansfield sisters; there would never be anyone like them again. Their spiritedness and singularity, the way rumours about them bred. How people grew preoccupied with them, how they dreaded and pursued them and might eventually ruin them. No other girls in history had ever met with such a fate.

He thought especially of Anne, and the fact that he had left her. Perhaps his expression gave him away, for Temperance was beside him now, squeezing his shoulder, and like a child he found his eyes filling with tears. "Sorry," he said, turning away. "I must go."

She walked with him to the door. When they stepped into the daylight, he noticed the lines around her mouth and eyes. "Here," he said, fumbling for some coins.

She shook her head. "Godspeed," she said, but her eyes weren't on the Greater Nettlebed road. She was looking backwards, down to the river, where Robin and Richard Wild-goose were walking up the path. They each carried a large brass pan, newly shined and gleaming in the sun.

"Always together, those two," she said.

The boys looked sombre and walked slowly, as though the pans were heavy.

"Good day," Robin said when they reached the road. He wouldn't meet Thomas's eye.

"All well?" Temperance asked.

Richard scowled. "Our hens are dead," he said. "Killed by dogs."

Thomas understood. Times were hard; they were pawning their pans.

"Stop in for some refreshment on your way home," Temperance said. "You too, Dickie—I won't tell your mother."

They watched them walk away—two stooping boys, blots on the brilliant road. Thomas saw Robin reach over to pat Richard's back and felt an unexpected pang. He thought of his own brothers and the times when they too had trudged to the pawnbrokers. He remembered the day he had left for Mansfield's farm, the new way his brothers looked at him. From that day, he had thought of himself in a new way too: as someone who would never again burden his parents, who stood on his own feet. He knew then that he wouldn't be going home that morning.

"Poor boys," Temperance said, arms crossed, squinting at

the receding pair. "It's not the dead hens that are the problem, it's their father's debts. Drinking," she said darkly. "And gambling. You know," she continued, "some say the Mansfields are responsible for the death of those hens."

Thomas's sweat-stained shirt rubbed unpleasantly on the back of his neck. He remembered Pete's warning in the alehouse on the day of his arrival in Little Nettlebed and thought of other conversations he had heard in the village and at the market. "Some say the Mansfields are responsible for a lot of things," he said.

She looked up at him. "Yes. They must be busy, those girls."

Opinions had a way of gathering and sticking, Thomas thought, like lines of ants swarming to honey. Every grievance found its way back to the sisters, it seemed.

So here was a second reason to stay in Little Nettlebed. He would forget what he had seen in the orchard and would stay to protect the sisters from the stories being told about them. Temperance, still watching him, smiled sadly. He thanked her again for the food and, turning his back to the homeward road, made his way to the ferry once more.

FIFTEEN

The ale was like a mother to him. It caressed his head and stroked his limbs. It whispered to him that he was clever and good, and he believed it. It led him to the edge of the river and laid him down, finding a tuffet of grass for his head. But there, listening to the soft tail-swishings of nearby cows and the trilling of insects, Pete Darling found that sleep would not come.

That day had been the last of his journeys across the Thames, he was sure of it. The river had narrowed—halfway across, at the water's deepest, he felt rough rock touch the underside of his ferry. The current, usually coursing and strong, had dwindled into a trickle. Tomorrow, people would be able to walk, and those going by cart would have to make the extra journey to the nearest bridge, several miles upstream. Little Nettlebed was no longer bounded by the river; instead, it was closed off by a bed of hard stone.

He had seen such a thing before, when his father was the ferryman: a hard, workless summer in the searing heat. But it was worse for Pete, much worse, because he was getting married next week. He felt uneasy about it, restless, and wanted someone to talk to. Temperance—whom he usually turned to for conversations of this sort—was being difficult, handing him pints with her prim, gloved hands, not meeting his eye. She was still annoyed about the Mansfield story.

He shook his head and tried to focus on the stars swimming above him. Did he wish he hadn't told that story? Perhaps, now. It had spread far beyond him, catching alight like a flare and carrying with a speed that startled him. But he had seen what he had seen, and now the vicar had seen it too, and Pete was glad that he and the vicar had been chosen as witnesses; it confirmed for him something important.

He tried to put it out of his mind, but often, when he'd had a few pints and found himself lying on the riverbank, the image appeared to him, of the five girls turning into dogs. Every time he returned to the memory of that evening—a memory so entrenched that he sometimes forgot how freshly minted it was, no more than a week old—he discovered something new, horrible details previously unseen. Their mouths overfilling with teeth; long, lolling tongues protruding from their lips. Unblinking eyes becoming large and amber, noses extending into snouts. What was smooth became hairy—yes, he remembered that now. Small hands grew claws and padded along the path. Their lilting chatter lowered into something wordless and deep. They were entirely transformed, and yet an impression was left of the girls they had been. In that brief moment, watching them across the water, Pete saw that they were still the Mansfield sisters. He could have identified them anywhere. The fierce one, the pretty one, the tomboy, the nervous one, the youngest. That was what had frightened him the most: they were not mere doltish dogs, they were girls with teeth and claws. Girls had crazy whims and grudges—these ones especially. He didn't trust them. They made him afraid.

He shifted. The stars continued to pool and play above him, and now the bank on which he lay began lifting and sinking too; everything was in motion but the unstirring riverbed below. He trembled his way to his feet and moved unsteadily among the tussocks to relieve himself. That was better. Now he'd be able to sleep. Turning, he saw a shape on the far bank, a figure. "Hail," he called, lifting his arm. The act unbalanced him, and he stumbled, lurching leftwards.

Recovering himself, he shouted again. "Hail!"

It was a boy, he noted gratefully. Not a girl, nor a dog. The boy had been crouching by the bulrushes and now rose to his feet.

"Who's there?" Pete called, his voice too loud in the quiet night air.

"Richard Wildgoose," said the boy. He sounded wary.

"Ah, yes. Robin's brother," Pete said, placing his hands on his hips. "I ferried you earlier."

"Yes."

They looked at each other for a few moments. Wildgoose's younger brother wasn't likely to make much of a companion, but Pete was lonely and wanted someone to listen to his woes. "Have you got anything to drink, lad?" he asked.

"No," Richard said, and crouched down again.

Pete blinked. "What are you doing there?"

"I'm looking at loaches. I'm trying to understand how they survive without water."

"In the dark?"

"In the daytime I have to help my mother at home. With the animals and suchlike." He paused, then continued conversationally: "Although now all our hens have been killed that's one less thing to look after, I suppose."

"Hens killed, eh?"

"Yes. We think by dogs." He seemed to notice Pete watching him, his hands still on his hips, and stood up again. "My mother thinks the Mansfield sisters did it, but Robin thinks that's nonsense. As for me, I haven't quite decided. I require a little more evidence."

Pete took an uneven step forward. "Things are getting out of hand with those girls, let me tell you." Another pause. "You know the vicar's seen it now? Those girls turning into dogs, I mean."

"The vicar?"

"Yes. No word of a lie, he saw it. In the orchard up at their farm. He told my future father-in-law, Humphrey Bullock, who told his daughter, who told me."

"Oh."

"I've seen it too. The change."

"I know."

"You know?"

"Everyone knows you saw it first, but not everyone believes your story. I thought I believed it, but then Robin told me I didn't." He cleared his throat, realising perhaps the childishness of what he'd just said. "But now the vicar has seen it I think Robin and I must believe it too."

"Robin didn't believe it at first?"

"No. He likes to gather proof."

"He does, does he?"

"Yes." Richard's chest became a barrel, manly and proud, daring Pete to tease him. "He's very fair. He's good at seeing the evidence. I bring him things I've heard, and he tells me whether they're true."

Pete staggered forward. "Sounds like Robin thinks he's God."

Richard's face became open and unhappy, a boy once more. "Oh, no! No, no, not at all."

"Listen to me, young Richard. Let me tell you something you'd do well to remember. The truth is like . . ."

He paused, uncertain. What was the truth like? He looked at the river for inspiration. The ale he'd been drinking fed words into his mouth. "The truth is like a water creature," he continued. "Too large for any single man to catch. He can take hold of one tentacle, or a silver tail, or a fin, but he'll never catch the whole creature, not on his own."

He put his hands in his pockets to try and stop the swaying. Yes, his speech had turned out nicely—he quite agreed with everything he'd said. "I tell you what: in future why don't you also come to me with all the things you've heard, and like your brother I'll tell you whether they're true. Then you'll have two men's opinions—much better than one."

Richard looked at him.

"And while you're at it, next time you're passing, maybe you can bring something to drink too. Then we can drink together and discuss the world like friends."

"Perhaps," Richard said eventually. He glanced at the dark road. "I'd better go now."

Pete watched his moonlit figure dwindle and disappear. He was alone again. He lowered himself down to the bank, fitting his body into the ground's hard grooves, and turned the encounter over in his mind. Why had he invited Robin's boy-brother to come to him with news? He wasn't sure. It irked him, perhaps, to think of weak, timid Wildgoose playing God in his home. If anyone was equipped to sort truth from untruth and right from wrong, it was Pete. Or no, he granted, maybe the vicar was foremost—but Pete came close behind. He had, after all, been acquainted with an angel, and was the first of the villagers to see the girls change. He was special. He could sniff the truth from a mile off. He was born with rightness in his bones.

But there was another motive too. If Richard came to him, Pete would know all that was happening in the village. He liked to hear what was going on; it was part of the reason he enjoyed his job so much. Ferrying the villagers across the river gave him access to their lives. People knew him, they trusted him, and to fill the brief journey from one bank to the other they opened their hearts to him. They told him about their sadness and their fear, their deep desires, their dull concerns. He was often the first to learn who'd lost what at cards, who was bedding whose wife. He knew exactly how people felt about their friends, their neighbours, the King. He liked to know. Possessing all that knowledge gave him a thrill.

Now he was ferryless and knowledgeless, all because of the heat. He groaned and then yelled, trying to volley his voice up into the heavens. "Where are you, rain?" he shouted, but the rain didn't respond, and Pete felt ashamed, because it was not the will of the rain that meant he was out of work, it was the will of God, and it was not for him to question God's will. He wiped salty tears from his cheeks and mouth and fell soundly asleep.

The sun didn't wake him, as it usually did; that morning it was a boot in his side. Above him, his face framed by brilliant blue sky, stood Humphrey Bullock. His skin was flushed and his mouth, when he opened it to speak, looked full of foaming spit. "What's the matter with you, Darling?" Bullock barked. "You've got a home, haven't you? Why don't you sleep there?"

Pete scrabbled to his feet. His head felt as though it was gripped in a giant's fist. "I'm sorry, sir. The evening ran away with me."

His brain began catching up with what he saw. Humphrey Bullock—here, on the far bank, unferried. He looked down at the river and found that his fears had been realised: it was only a few yards wide now, and so low that a person could wade through it without trouble. Bullock's trousers had barely been touched by water.

"You walked?"

Bullock scowled at him. "I walked. You can tie up your punt for the season. The village has no use for a ferryman."

"I have money, sir. A nest-egg. All will be well."

"I should hope so."

They eyed each other with dislike. Pete saw in Bullock something of his future bride: a certain softness of chin and downturn of mouth. He looked away.

"Were you merely passing?"

Bullock snorted. "No, funnily enough, I was not *merely passing*. I came to find you. Something told me you wouldn't be far from the Swan."

He cocked his thumb at the gate up to the alehouse.

"I've been hearing things, Darling. You've been drinking too much, you've been picking fights. And then there's the matter of the stories about the Mansfield girls."

Pete frowned down at him. "Sir?"

"These stories . . . I think it's best if you distance yourself from them. Focus on the wedding instead."

"But sir—they aren't stories. It's the truth. You know it yourself—you've heard it from the vicar."

Bullock's face tightened. "I expect Agnes told you about my audience with Reverend Kennett, although it's really none of your business." He took a square of linen from his pocket and wiped his forehead. "The vicar is a friend of mine, and, yes, I heard his report about the Mansfield sisters." He cleared his throat quietly. "It's a difficult time for the church, what with all these new ideas about . . . Well, ideas of science and so on, and, frankly, if he wants to go around talking about the devil and such, then I believe he has every right to do so." He wiped his brow again. "But I don't think it behoves a modern young man, a man with *learning* and . . . and . . . *prospects* to peddle such stories."

Pete's thoughts wandered as his future father-in-law spoke. He was thinking about the dream he'd had, of Agnes as Eve, the dream that had told him she was the woman he should marry. A realisation was dawning on him: perhaps he had been wrong about the dream. Perhaps the dream was not a message from God, as he had supposed, but was in fact merely a dream, the consequence of too much cheese and ale and sleeping rough on the riverbank. The idea felt like lice crawling over his skin.

Maybe Bullock saw something in Pete's expression that he didn't like. He took a step towards him, so that their faces were close; Bullock's breath tasted sweet, like candied fruit. "Nothing can go wrong for my daughter, do you hear me? You will be the perfect husband to her, faithful and hard-working. You will drink only in moderation. And you will stop spreading stories about those sisters, however repellent you might find them to be." A vein pulsed in his temple. "Do I make myself clear?"

Pete nodded and swallowed.

"Good," Bullock said and, without a word of parting, strode out across the sun-scorched river.

SIXTEEN

HAYMAKING WAS A HAPPY TIME FOR ROBIN. HE LIKED THE smell of the drying grass, the pleasant-painful ache in his arms and back at the end of each day, the first swig of ale when they stopped at noon to eat. He didn't think during haymaking; he was mindless, a machine. He preferred to be that way.

During haymaking, he was accountable to no one but the fields and the air. He didn't worry about the men, or what they made of him, and the men seemed not to worry about him. The long days of searing labour exhausted them—there wasn't space for anything more. Their weariness was Robin's close ally; they couldn't spare the strength to concern themselves with him.

At dawn, Robin left his cottage for the great open fields that bordered the village to the south. The birds sang from the hedgerows, and the wood pigeons murmured, and the sun sent bright haloes of light around each lobed oak leaf above him. It was a good day to be alive, and Robin ran down the path and along the road to Mansfield's farm. Turning in at the gate, he slowed, cautious in case he encountered one of the girls, but that morning there was no sign of them. Some of them might be at the fields already or would come down later with their dinner; he would see them then. He collected his scythe and continued on his way, along the road where it narrowed into a track towards the fields.

There he began his work, rocking the scythe in clean arcs back and forth, and soon the other village lads joined, and Thomas, and even Mansfield himself, although he worked slowly now and rested often. Observing Mansfield in his broad-brimmed hat, leaning on his upturned scythe, Robin thought he looked older, smaller, his back rounded into a constant hunch. He remembered what his mother had said over breakfast, about feeling sorry for the old man, what with these rumours going around and his wife being dead and all. But Robin had detected a note of satisfaction in her voice, and if he had been pressed for the truth he would have to say that in his view his mother wasn't sorry at all; in fact, she seemed almost glad that the Mansfields were suffering this misfortune. After all, she might have said, there was a time when those in Little Nettlebed had suffered—even the Mansfields' closest neighbours—and the old man hadn't done a thing.

Now it was their turn to suffer, and their suffering was all the villagers talked about. After the vicar saw the change, others started seeing it too—always at a distance, across fields or the river, or in the thin dusk light. Robin heard these stories from Richard and told him to disbelieve them all (especially the ones—for there were a few—in which people claimed to have seen the sisters turn into a creature closely resembling the blacksmith's dog, a terrier named Mischief). Church had been busier than usual on Sunday, full of people hoping to see if the girls would change mid-service, would sink their fangs into the hassocks or lap up the communion wine. Even the vicar had sent the sisters odd glances, and his sermon about casting out the devil seemed addressed directly to them. But they had disappointed everybody by doing nothing, by sitting demurely and bowing their heads in prayer. If the devil was within them, it appeared that more would be required to cast him out.

Not everyone believed that the girls were being changed by the devil; the villagers' beliefs differed but were all firmly held. In every theory was an undercurrent of fear. What if the girls' condition spread, like a pox? What if they tore people apart with those long, pointed teeth, or killed their livestock? What if they drove everyone out of the village? What if they set up a terrible dog dominion, where people lived in servitude? It struck Robin, listening to Richard reel off these questions, that the villagers were more afraid of the girls themselves than they were of the dogs. Girls—normal human girls—people could contend with; they were weak and small. And dogs too could be trained. But girls who became dogs, or who let the world believe they were dogs, were either powerful or mad: both monstrous possibilities.

As a result of all this, one or two of the boys who usually helped Mansfield with the haymaking were absent this year. Both Robin and his mother agreed that this was silly, though for different reasons. (No amount of devilry or pox-spreading could convince Mistress Wildgoose that forgoing a few weeks' pay was a good idea.) So here Robin was, despite the rumours, and he was soon to be fed his dinner by the girls themselves, the first time he'd seen them face-to-face since this had all started.

He settled into a rhythm, Thomas beside him, and allowed the thoughts of sisters and of dogs to leave his mind; now all he knew was the task at hand. He felt the sun burning the back of his neck and the handle of the scythe rubbing against his palms. He smelled the sweet scent of cut grass. He heard

Thomas's breath, ragged and low. They worked without a break until late morning, when Mansfield called for them to stop. Robin stretched, forcing his aching back to straighten. He narrowed his eyes to see which of the girls was bringing their food—usually it was Anne and Elizabeth, but sometimes Grace helped too. (Hester only came when she was permitted to pick up a scythe herself, something her grandfather no longer allowed her to do. She'd been denied that privilege last year after dropping one in delight at the sight of Mary arriving at the field with Catchrat; Catchrat, falling like spilled milk from Mary's arms, almost lost a tail.)

They gathered in the shade and waited. Some of the boys made quiet jokes to each other and tittered. Robin realised that they were all apprehensive; that, like him, they were awaiting the arrival of the girls, sending quick, darting looks over their shoulders at the track to see if they were approaching. At last, a pair of figures did approach, two girls carrying baskets. But Robin could see, even from a distance, that the hair pinned neatly beneath their caps was golden, that they were short and plump, not tall and thin as Anne was. They reached the field, and Robin heard a soft exhalation from the boys, a sigh—perhaps of disappointment, or possibly of relief. It was Connie and Amie who'd brought their lunch, not the Mansfield sisters; they handed out bread and cheese and ale, and whatever tension had been hanging in the dry summer air was broken. The boys spoke normally again, and Thomas asked Robin about his plans after haymaking, and Robin answered and ate. It was only old Mansfield who didn't seem to relax.

Robin watched Mansfield eat. He saw how the old man's hand searched for the bread in his lap, and how it trembled slightly as he lifted the food to his mouth; he remembered again his mother's gleeful tone and felt unhappy. He was staring at Mansfield, pitying him, when Mansfield turned and looked directly at him. Robin stopped eating and stood, skin tingling, as though to stretch his legs, and Mansfield's eyes seemed to follow him up. Unnerved, Robin lowered himself back down, the old man's eyes still on him. It was as if Mansfield could see him, something Robin believed to be impossible. Yet stranger things had happened. In a world where girls turned into dogs, a blind man suddenly being able to see felt almost ordinary.

After the food was finished, they returned to work. The warmth and the ale made Robin unsteady. The other lads felt it too, the sun's oppressive weight. One boy described how his elderly aunt had fainted the day before, just suddenly dropping to the ground like an apple falling from a tree. It was the heat, the boy said darkly. It wore people down.

They were sombre for a moment, but the mood was short-lived, and their chatter soon led elsewhere. Moving through the field, Robin heard one of the boys mutter a joke about wanting to give a village girl a green gown (which he took to mean something about lying on the grass, although he wasn't entirely sure), and he laughed as though it were funny. Maybe that was all it took: a cup of ale, a shared joke, and now he was one of them. He got back into the rhythm of the work and again his mind cleared; he felt only the aches in his back, the blisters rubbing on his hands, and the hot sun beating down on his body.

One of the boys, Walter, fell in time beside him, and they worked together for a while, their laboured breath in conversation. Robin had known Walter since boyhood; they'd often played together by the river, or up on the brow of the hill in Greater Nettlebed, watching for hawks. Since then, they'd drifted, their lives looping away from each other. And perhaps it had only been that—drifting—but Robin suspected Walter had seen something in him he didn't like, a glimpse of a difference. Shame spread over him like a rash.

Sometimes, though, the meaning of difference shifted. Walter smiled at Robin when he first arrived that morning and sat beside him while they ate. Now here he was, working next to him, clearing his throat as though he was about to speak. "I'm guessing you've heard about Mansfield's granddaughters, then," he said in a low voice.

Robin continued working, swinging his scythe low to the ground. He cast a quick look at the far side of the field, where the old man was toiling. "I have," he said.

"Crazy, isn't it," Walter said. "I was hoping we'd catch a glimpse of them today." He grinned at Robin. "Did you hear that they've now been spotted in Greater Nettlebed, as well?"

Robin swallowed and said nothing.

"What?" Walter said, stopping his work and looking at Robin. "Don't tell me you feel sorry for them."

Robin stopped too and looked at Walter. How easy it would be to tell Walter he didn't feel sorry for the girls, that he'd also heard they'd been seen in Greater Nettlebed, that in fact he'd seen them himself, loping along the riverbank, barking and flea-bitten, baring yellow teeth. It would be the antidote to so much misery, the cure for his uneasy difference. He preferred the truth—of course he did. But in that moment, it felt tempting—almost fatally painless—to say these words that would fix so many of his problems. He was seduced by Walter's coaxing look and forgot all about the lesson he'd so recently tried to teach Richard about telling the truth. He could do it, he thought, moistening his lips. He could do it. He could—

Thomas strode up beside them. "Why have you stopped?"

Robin shook his head. He couldn't do it. Walter picked up his scythe and spat. "We were just talking about the Mansfield sisters. Mansfield bitches, I should say. Wildgoose feels sorry for them."

Robin caught Thomas's eye and saw there not intrigue or disgust but something close to sympathy. He blinked and looked away.

"What do you make of it all, Mildmay?" Walter said. "You must have seen some things, living in the grounds."

Thomas was hunched over his scythe, sweat beading on his temple. Robin thought he saw the tips of his ears burning. "I haven't seen anything," Thomas said. "There's nothing wrong with those girls."

Walter swung his blade. "Nonsense! You must have seen or heard something. Unnameable noises late at night. Scratchings at the door." He snickered, breathless.

"There's nothing wrong with those girls," Thomas said again. Robin admired his steadiness, the way he withstood Walter's goads. "Master Mansfield's getting a doctor to visit from Oxford, to snuff out the rumours."

Walter whistled and drew back his scythe. "A doctor, eh? Must be something, then. You don't just call out a doctor for nothing."

Thomas shook his head, and Robin saw that the flush had overcome his face. "He wants to prove to the vicar, to everyone who's been asking questions, that there's nothing wrong with the girls. The doctor will find nothing. They're perfectly well."

Walter scoffed. "We'll see about that," he said.

They didn't speak much after that, silenced by the blazing sun and the grass and the weight of the scythes. When they finished working, Robin saw Walter report the news about the doctor to the other boys. Their eyes widened, and they whispered to each other, but Robin, not wanting to be drawn into their conversation, turned away from them and didn't hear what was said; he walked instead with Mansfield back to the farm to return his scythe. The old man said nothing along the way. In the yard, he reached up and touched his own head.

"Oh, Wildgoose," he said, frowning. "I've left my hat back in the field. I'll be needing it tomorrow. Would you run and retrieve it for me?"

"Of course," Robin said, eyeing the house, sorry not to have seen the girls.

The sun was joined by a crescent moon in the shimmering sky. The birdsong had quietened; stillness closed in. Robin was glad to be alone. He wouldn't go down to the alehouse that evening. Talking to Walter, he'd found a weakness in himself that worried him. For a moment, he saw how he could become like everyone else. He could make things up, feeding the villagers' appetites for stories about the sisters and their odd, demonic ways. Perhaps he would even start believing his own tales. Lies could be told with such liberating ease—they tasted better on the tongue than hard facts. But Robin didn't want to become like the other villagers, a story-spreader, fitting easily into the crowd. He wanted to stay faithful to the truth.

A pair of ravens, vivid against the pale sky, swooped overhead. He stopped abruptly, remembering the supernatural knack these birds had for sensing death. He couldn't explain it, but he had seen them before, roosting on the homes of those whose time on earth was ending. He bowed his head. Maybe they wouldn't settle in Little Nettlebed today. He prayed that they were simply passing through.

Mansfield's hat was by the stump on which he had taken his rest earlier. Robin picked it up, and then sat down on the stump himself, closing his eyes and breathing in the smell of the still-warm ground. The scythed grass had been raked into rows, drying in the sun. At the far edge of the field, the uncut grass whispered and rustled; it sounded like voices. He opened his eyes. Yes—voices. It was unmistakable: those of a man and a woman. He squinted and saw—beyond the grass, tucked beside a copse of trees—two figures facing each other. Like night and day they were, the man in a loose white shirt with golden curls, the woman in a black dress, her dark hair pinned from her face. Robin could make out Thomas, but he wasn't sure about the woman. She looked familiar. He narrowed his eyes. No, he thought, shaking his head. It couldn't be.

He stayed on the stump, realising that, with the tall grasses and the growing shadows, he was concealed from the pair. He didn't want to deceive them but seemed somehow unable to get up and go; he was fixed to the spot, watching. He saw Thomas reach towards the woman. He saw him touch her hand, running his fingers along the back of hers. He saw him graze the cuff of her dress. He saw her look at him, a long steady look. They had stopped speaking, it seemed, or perhaps Robin could no longer hear them.

A few years earlier, when Richard was a small boy, Robin had found him staring at the sun, tears seeping down his plump cheeks. "Dickie!" he'd said, shaking him. "Don't look at it!"

His brother had turned to him, dazed.

"You could hurt yourself doing that. You could make yourself blind."

Richard was silent, staring, blinking.

"Are you well? Can you see?"

"Yes, Robin," Richard said in a small voice. "I can see."

"Why did you do it?"

Richard bit his lip, a child. "It just looked so bright and beautiful. I couldn't look away."

It had pained Robin, his brother's innocence. And now here he was himself: staring, blinking, innocent. He couldn't look away.

He shook his head. He shouldn't watch this. Crouching, Mansfield's hat crumpling in his fist, he made his way back to the track.

Away from the field, he breathed heavily. It was strange, what he had seen. If Richard had reported it to him as something he'd heard in the village, he would have told his brother that it was impossible. An untruth. For the man and the woman looked as though they were in love, and it wasn't possible for this particular man and woman to be in love. Not Thomas, who always seemed so good and rule-abiding. Not with Anne. He was sure of it now: the way the woman stood; her tight, strained expression; her black dress. He kicked the stubbled grass and began to run, a feeling of dread building in his chest. He hoped that no one would ever hear about this. He couldn't bear to think how it would sound in the villagers' mouths. Yes, they'd tell each other, the devil's at work again—the new farmhand, so guileless and sweet, has been seduced by the eldest dog-sister.

SEVENTEEN

IT WAS GRACE WHO HAD TOLD THOMAS ABOUT THE doctor's visit, a furtive confession; the family wouldn't discuss such a thing in front of others. Though the girls talked without stopping through every meal, they never let anything of significance slip, gossiping instead, or teasing one another, or making up fictions about pirate ships. Anne and old Mansfield talked over matters of household importance alone—Thomas knew this already. But there were other things that happened in private. Sometimes, the sound of crying carried down to him from the upstairs windows. He found the girls gathered in corners, talking in hushed voices. He saw Mansfield pacing slowly up and down in the parlour and knew that something was worrying him.

Connie had a better understanding of these things (she wasn't above pressing her ear to certain doors). She reported what she knew to Thomas and Amie, who gathered like a congregation at church to hear what she had to say. Her sermons consisted of pieced-together snippets, snatches of eavesdropped conversations. Thomas didn't believe them fully, but still he liked to find out what she had gleaned. Any information was better than none.

The Mansfield sisters were a fortress. Despite all the time he spent with them, standing among them in the garden, or walking with them to church, or eating with them, or praying with them, or talking with Anne, he knew he would never truly know them. Even when Mary had made him stay awake one moonless night the week before, to see if the moon people ("Your kin!" she'd announced happily) would alight on earth for dancing and revelry—they had lain on the hayrick, where the other girls eventually joined them—even then, keeping a laughing watch together, he had known that he was a foreigner. They were separate to him, impenetrable. They spoke their own language, which consisted of no English words at all but was communicated through looks and movement alone. Early on, he'd tried to make a glossary in his mind; he noted each hair toss, each playful pinch, each sigh. But the list was too long, the meanings too subtle. He felt stupid. He gave up trying to understand.

Sometimes he thought they hated him. They were cold and dismissive. They stole his clothes when he bathed. They turned on their heels and left without warning. Sometimes he felt tolerated. Only once, in that miraculous encounter in the hayfield with Anne, did he feel truly loved, but she grew stiff in the company of the others. He reconciled himself to his fate: he would wait patiently, for a lifetime if necessary, for them to accept him. They could take him or leave him as they pleased.

For the most part it pleased them to leave him, but one day he found Grace skulking nearby while he fed the horses. The others often ignored him, but Grace never did; he felt the constant burn of her eyes on his face. She was wary of everyone, and he was no exception. “Good day, Miss Grace,” he said.

He’d embarrassed her—she blushed and retreated. Soon, though, he found her at the stable door again, her arms folded around herself worriedly.

“Can I help you with anything?”

She shook her head. Her eyes were wide and sad. Thomas put down the sack he had been holding and looked at her for a long time. He’d tried so hard to learn the sisters’ language; now was his chance to make use of his lessons. “There’s something troubling you, isn’t there, Miss Grace?”

She didn’t speak. Her right foot shifted inward.

“But you’re scared to talk about it. Maybe someone told you not to?”

She looked at the floor, then back at his face.

“I see. And you want to talk to me because . . . because I’m outside of the family?”

Her mouth twitched.

“Maybe because I spend time in the village?”

She paused, then nodded.

“You’re wondering if I’ve heard something in the village?”

She nodded again.

“Something about your family, perhaps?”

She bit her lip, then cleared her throat. “Yes,” she said.

He blinked. “I see,” he said.

“Your face tells me you *have* heard something in the village. Tell me what you’ve heard.”

He tried to smile at her. “There are rumours going around about every family in this land. You mustn’t pay them any attention.”

She took a step forward. "I know what they're saying. I just wanted to hear you say it." Her hand toyed nervously with her dress. "Grandfather's received a letter from someone in Oxford. A doctor. He's heard all about us, it seems, and wants to pay us a visit. He wants to find out about our *condition*." She eyed him as she said the word. "Grandfather's agreed. He hopes to be able to tell everyone that there isn't anything wrong with us, that this doctor himself says so."

Thomas contemplated her as she spoke. His heartbeat quickened. "Please forgive me for asking, Miss Grace. But *is* there . . ."

"Is there what?" she said. "Anything wrong with us?"

He nodded, ashamed.

Her face seemed suddenly very old. "Oh," she said. "So much."

He laughed awkwardly, but he wasn't ready to let the matter go. Every time he'd seen Anne, he'd wanted to ask her about it. He wished he didn't need to. He wished there was no doubt in his mind that the stories weren't true. "So you're all . . . quite well? It's just . . ." He paused. "I was here when the vicar visited. I saw what he saw."

She looked at him coolly, her nervousness gone. "And what did you see?"

"I saw . . ." He swallowed and crossed his arms. "I thought I saw . . . I thought, for a moment, that I saw Anne's—*Miss* Anne's—face change. I thought I saw a change come upon her."

"Have you asked Anne about this change?"

"No," he said, shaking his head. "No. It's not my place."

"I'll be sorry if you've told this story in the village, Thomas."

The way she said it—the tone, the tilt of her head—gave her the appearance of a woman of fifty.

"I would never do so," he said and bowed his head towards her.

"Good," she said and bit her lip again. "I'm sorry. I'm just worried. The others . . . They don't realise what will happen if the doctor finds anything out of the ordinary. They think it's just a game."

"No," he said. "Surely not."

"No," she agreed. "I suppose not. Not a game. More like a battle—a battle they want to win."

She was so young, Thomas thought, looking at her. She was a child. Everything was meant to be a game still; the battles would come later. She touched the hair around her face and fiddled with her cap, nervous again.

Speaking casually, as though he didn't care what answer she gave, he asked: "And what will your sisters say to the doctor?"

He held his breath. She frowned and looked at the floor. "I don't know."

"Grace," he said. "It's not for me to tell you what to do, I know. Please forgive me for speaking out of turn. But your sisters need to be careful." He looked at her closely, saw her mouthing something to herself, her hands wrestling with each other. "You asked me what people are saying in the village, so I'll tell you. Some people think you've been possessed by demons. Some say you're mad, others that you have a terrible disease brought over on a boat from France. A great many want you to leave. They are very fearful."

He heard her give a small sob, and he stopped. "I'm sorry, I didn't mean to frighten you. I just want you to be careful. Please tell the others what you've heard."

She took a step back. "I should go. Thank you, Thomas."

He watched her leave. His heart was at once light and full of worry. The girls were in danger. The girls had let him in.

* * *

A FEW DAYS later, when the doctor arrived, Thomas was anxious and unslept. The clattering of hooves in the yard summoned him outside, where he found a man trying to settle his mare. The man looked young; his face was boyishly unbearded. Maybe, Thomas thought, stepping forward and taking the mare's bridle, he was still a student at the university. The thought disconcerted him. He had hoped the sisters would be seen by someone older, more distinguished, a physician with many years of learning who would immediately identify what—if anything—was wrong with them. He didn't feel such confidence in the young man before him, who dismounted eagerly and gave the house a hungry look. "Thank you, lad," he said. "My name's John Friend. I'm here to examine the girls. They're inside, I take it?"

Thomas's stomach churned. "Yes, sir," he said.

"Rumours have reached me in Oxford—stories about these girls," the doctor said in a low voice. "I've heard they're like a pack of hounds. I wanted to see for myself. Tell me, boy, have you seen it?"

Thomas glanced up at the house. All five sisters were watching him from the windows. Hester had drawn whiskers on her face with charcoal. He shook his head.

"Nothing?"

"No, sir. They are normal girls."

Mansfield, appearing at the door, came forward to greet the doctor, and Thomas led the mare to the stable. He wished he could know what was happening inside the house. Connie and Amie were out at the market; he had no way of discovering what would take place between the girls and the doctor. Anne, he knew, would never tell him, for although he now believed himself to have earned her trust, she couldn't shed the fetters of her pride.

He took the horse to the trough, patting her distractedly on the rump while she drank, then tied her up and waited, searching the warm air for sound. He felt brittle with worry. In that moment, he wasn't a man. He was fine Venetian glass of the type Elizabeth dreamed of drinking from one day, capable of shattering. His eyes grew tired from staring at the windows. No voices reached him—no sound at all. He stood alone in the dusty yard and filled the silence with thoughts of Anne. Anne. It was amazing to him, and mystifying, and frightening, and wonderful that Anne returned his love for her. Perhaps she had noticed his absence that day when he'd set out for his home, or maybe she had sensed, since then, the deepening of his devotion. He wasn't sure what it was, but something had swayed her. She was now his. And though he understood that it couldn't last, he was happy. Even knowing she was nearby, within those walls, thrilled him. He could think of her all day long and not be bored. He could gladly think—

A sound startled him out of his reverie. Someone was shouting inside the house. Who? Why? He moved swiftly across the yard, stopping beneath the window. He could hear better now. He listened and discovered that it wasn't shouting at all. It was a sound he couldn't put a word to. Not crying, not really. More like howling. *Like a pack of hounds*, the doctor had said; that's what this sounded like. The howling of a pack of hounds.

Thomas was shaking. He heard the doctor ask the girls if

they knew where they were. He heard Mansfield speak. "Girls!" he said, his voice cracking. "I beg your pardon, Doctor—I don't know what's got into them. Girls, stop this right now!"

Thomas pressed his back to the brick, horror building in his throat. It was too late; there was nothing he could do to help them. The doctor would go away and write up what he had witnessed. He would tell the world about the Mansfield sisters—how they turned into dogs, just as everybody said. And now Thomas had no choice but to concede it might be true. Why else were the girls howling? What other explanation could there be for the thing he'd seen in the orchard that day?

The sisters continued to howl, and the doctor, excited now, continued asking them questions. Thomas could hear, somewhere in the mix, the sound of groaning—Mansfield, it must be. It was almost as if the girls were speaking to each other; they howled in turn, responding to their sisters, their voices rising. At last, the terrible chorus subsided. Somewhere above Thomas, a bee or a moth flew over and over against the windowpane, trying to get free. The tapping grew louder. When he looked up, he saw Mansfield standing there, his thin arthritic finger sounding against the glass.

Thomas needed no further encouragement. He raced inside, his eyes adjusting to the dim light, and up the stairs. He followed the doctor's voice to the room where the girls were being examined. Stepping in, he saw the sisters—all of them—lying in a heap on the floor. They were awake, but the blood seemed to have drained from their faces; they were pale, and their eyes were circled by dark rings. They rested their heads on each other's shoulders and stomachs and watched him stand in the doorway.

"Quite extraordinary," the doctor was saying.

"Mildmay, is that you?" Mansfield said, his eyes wild. "Help the girls to their rooms, will you? They are hysterical. They must have rest."

"Yes, sir," Thomas said and stepped towards the girls. He picked up Mary first, who gave him a disgusted look, as though she was being torn too early from a game. He carried her out into the corridor. She was light: a doll. "Where's your bedroom, Mary?" he asked.

She gestured noncommittally to the door opposite, and Thomas carried her in and placed her on the bed, pulling a coverlet over her. He carried Hester (rigid) and Grace (trembling) into the room they shared with Mary, while the doctor looked on, and Mansfield groaned, and the other girls watched him from the floor. He came back for Elizabeth (blushing) and carried her into a separate room—the room she shared with Anne. But there was no time to look at it, no time to wonder at the tapestries hanging around the bed, or the dip Anne's body had made in the feather mattress. He returned to the first room, where the doctor had just finished taking Anne's pulse, and picked her up. Her hands on his shoulders were hot. Her face was very close to his.

"Why did you do it?" he whispered in the corridor.

She looked at him and smiled.

He placed her on the bed beside Elizabeth and stood there for a moment. He wanted to ask them what had happened, but he knew he couldn't, that he wouldn't understand their answer anyhow. The girls lay on their sides, facing each other, and they held both the other's hands. They didn't speak, but they were saying something—Thomas's lessons in the girls' language hadn't got far enough for him to know what it was.

He returned to the men and stood in the doorway, listening.

"The girls have been up to some mischief, sir," Mansfield was saying. "There is nothing wrong with them, upon my soul."

The doctor was no longer the animated young man Thomas had met outside; he seemed suddenly very grave. "That is not my impression at all, sir. The girls are clearly suffering, although I don't believe them to be in any danger. Their pulses are fine, perhaps a little weakened at the end, and they seem to be in full possession of their faculties. It resembles other cases I've heard about, other hysteric disorders. It is my belief that animal spirits are producing disturbances in their nerves, contracting their muscles and so forth."

Mansfield gaped. "Animal spirits?"

"Oh, nothing supernatural, I assure you. There are three kinds of spirit within the body: animal, vital, and natural. Animal spirits create movement and feeling. They're carried by the nerves." He paused. "In my opinion, the girls are suffering from a nervous disorder caused by erratic animal spirits. It's possible that it began in one or two of them, and the others are imitating the condition."

Mansfield staggered forward and touched the doctor's sleeve. "But Doctor . . . What do you suggest we do? How will the girls recover?"

"They need rest, sir. I can also give you a list of food they should eat. But rest is the most important thing."

He leaned in towards Mansfield. Thomas lingered in the doorway; the old man had clearly forgotten he was there, and he was determined to hear what the doctor had to say.

"It is believed that the animal spirits can be disturbed by all sorts of things. Finding oneself threatened or in danger can make the movements of the animal spirits irregular. The sight of something frightening can have the same effect."

"Their beloved grandmother died recently," Mansfield murmured. "It could be the shock of that."

"Indeed," the doctor said. "Although—forgive me for saying so—but if you alone are their guardian, sir, and there's one of you, and five of them, and your sight is poor, there are many things they might have seen or experienced without your knowledge."

"What do you mean?"

"Nothing. Forgive the suggestion. I merely mean that girls can get themselves into trouble, that's all. I would suggest, for the sake of their health, that you keep them inside and have your servants watch them until they are calmed and recovered."

Thomas breathed in sharply.

"Mildmay?" Mansfield said, lifting his face towards him. "Are you still here? Begone with you, boy. Out!"

Thomas retreated, making his way through the house and out into the garden. Was it true, all this talk about animal spirits and convulsions? Weren't the girls just play-acting, as they'd done so often before? He thought back to the change he had seen the day the vicar visited. At least now he knew that had been an illusion; it had scared him, and he thought about it often. The way Anne's face had looked . . . It was not the face of the girl he loved. But he had been wrong, and the vicar was wrong, and all the others who claimed they'd seen the sisters turn into dogs were wrong as well. He felt unexpectedly hopeful. Yes, he would be sorry not to see Anne while she was confined inside, but there was much to be glad about. The rumours weren't true: she wasn't possessed. She needed rest, that was all—and after that, all would be well.

EIGHTEEN

When the doctor left, Joseph called Thomas, and together they lifted large pieces of furniture from the parlour to the corridor upstairs. A heavy chest was placed against the door to Hester, Grace, and Mary's room. Outside Anne and Elizabeth's room they put a tall walnut armchair. "Please don't strain yourself, Grandfather," Anne said through the door. "We're not going to try to get out."

But the old man didn't respond; he was shaken up and deeply unhappy with the girls. He couldn't bear to speak to them.

"Go now, Mildmay," he said. "Don't tell anyone what has taken place today. And when Connie and Amie return from the market, please send them in right away. They'll need to watch over my granddaughters."

Alone, he sat in the chair where Anne attended to his eyes every morning and felt the tears drip down his nose. The girls were at fault, but he was too. He had let them down; he had allowed them to be broken. His wife would never have let this happen. She would have protected them. There would be no disturbed spirits, no nervous disorders, if she'd been alive.

He had only ever thought of his granddaughters as beautiful and bold, but the doctor had told him they were wounded in some way, that they needed rest. This distressed him greatly. He didn't like to think of them as fragile. He searched within his soul and saw a terrible truth: that he'd rather they were dogs than damaged girls. Dogs lived ignorantly and happily; they didn't know the extent of human pain. He wanted to preserve them from all the fears and the threats with which life might present them.

Voices sounded in the garden. It was a shock to hear cheerfulness and laughter when the house was so still. He heard nothing from the upstairs rooms. A lowered voice spoke outside—Thomas's, he supposed—and the cheerful voices grew grave. He heard footsteps in the passage and a knock at the door. "Come in," he said.

"Good afternoon, sir," Connie said. "We've just returned from the market, and Thomas told us of the doctor's visit. He says you'd like us to watch over your granddaughters."

"Thank you, Connie. Yes, the girls have suffered a nervous attack. Nothing to worry about, but they require plenty of rest. They must remain in their rooms until they're fully recovered. It's imperative that they don't leave the house until they're better."

A silence followed, which Joseph found impossible to interpret. He looked closely at them but couldn't make out their expressions.

"Is that clear, Connie? For now, perhaps one of you can keep watch while the other prepares supper."

Another silence. Joseph searched it for meaning. He peered at the girls but could see nothing at all in the bleary doorway: no motion, no shape. Gradually, he found that the silence was being filled by hushed sounds, the quiet movement of lips and the clicking of tongues. He realised the girls were mouthing things to each other. He listened, curious, as the soft mouthings expanded into whispers and finally into a single spoken word. "No," Connie said firmly.

"What did you say?"

"I'm very sorry, sir. I truly am. You've been so kind to me and my sister over the years, but I've got to think about our health first. I'm sorry but I must. Amie almost died in childhood. I can't go through anything of that sort ever again."

He looked at them, but still saw nothing. "I don't follow."

"This attack that the young ladies have experienced. Convulsions and such like—spreading from one to the next. We can't risk catching it ourselves. We don't want to get into any trouble."

More whispering ensued. The sisters didn't seem to agree.

"No, Amie," Connie hissed. "I won't have it. We don't know anything about this illness. If the doctor said the young ladies must be contained, I don't believe we should be watching them and feeding them and so on. It isn't safe."

The room started to sway; Joseph felt storm-tossed, adrift. He gripped the arms of his chair. "If you won't go near the girls then I don't believe you can stay here."

Amie let out a stifled sob.

"Very well, sir. We'll leave in the morning," Connie said.

Joseph thought he could hear in her voice, beneath the bravado, something fearful and small. He softened. "Where will you go?"

"We have a cousin in London, a maid in the house of a wealthy gentleman. We'll see if she can help us find work."

"I'll give you something for your journey."

"Thank you, sir. We appreciate everything you and our late mistress have done for us, truly."

He nodded, gripping his chair tighter. He heard the rustling of skirts—a curtsy—and their retreating steps. Then returning footsteps and a gentle knock at the door. "Sir?"

It was Amie this time, her voice quavering.

"Yes, Amie?"

"I would be very grateful, if it's not too much trouble, if you could tell the young ladies something from me."

Joseph raised his eyebrows. "It's no trouble."

"Thank you, sir. If you could give them all my fondest wishes, I would be much obliged. And please thank Miss Anne for all her kindness over the years. And please tell Miss Elizabeth that if we ever meet again, I shall tell her about all the fine dresses I see while I'm in London. And please tell Miss Grace that she is a very good child, and Miss Hester that she is a very naughty one whom I shall dearly miss." Her voice began to crack. "And please tell Miss Mary that I'll miss her too, and that I'll be keeping all of them in my prayers."

She broke off; Joseph heard her crying.

"There, there," he said awkwardly, reaching into his pocket for a handkerchief. "The girls will miss you very much too, Amie. I'll make sure to pass on your messages."

"Thank you, sir," she said, blowing her nose. "I'm very sorry to be leaving you. You've been so kind to us, and we won't ever forget it."

"Very good. Thank you, Amie."

She blew her nose again and left. Alone in the swaying parlour, he reckoned up the household. One old man and five granddaughters, one farmhand and no maids. He would have to go to the fair to find someone to replace the girls, but there would be difficulties, he knew. Even if word hadn't got out about the rumours and the doctor's visit, the world would now be certain that something was wrong at the Mansfield house; loyal maidservants didn't leave for no reason. The departure of Connie and Amie was proof that there was some kind of trouble and was sure to incite further stories. It was necessary for the girls to stay inside until the villagers lost interest, which he hoped wouldn't be far in the future. There would soon be something new to fear.

The maids prepared supper, which Joseph himself took up to his granddaughters' rooms, bowl by bowl, while Thomas removed the furniture and opened the doors.

"I'm very sorry to tell you this, girls," Joseph said, standing in the corridor, "but Connie and Amie are leaving in the morning. You will not have the chance to say goodbye to them."

He heard gasps and tears. Someone threw something soft; it met the wall with a sigh. "Grandfather," Anne said. "Please."

He shook his head. "Thomas will be keeping watch. It's for your own good."

He felt his way back along the corridor and into the parlour, which had stilled. He sat in his chair until he heard the candle burn out and the singeing scent filled his nostrils. He sat there, unsleeping, until he heard the first cock crow at dawn.

By breakfast, the day was bakingly hot; standing in the yard, saying goodbye to Connie and Amie, Joseph felt as though he were in a furnace, or the hellfire about which the vicar warned them each week. He discerned the outline of the girls, saw them walk away for the last time. Soon they blurred and disappeared, and he heard the gate swing open. Behind him came sounds from the upstairs windows. Unmaidenly sounds; they pained him. Wailing—was that Mary?—and Grace's little whimpers. He went inside and didn't emerge again that day.

As noon approached, he felt his way upstairs and tapped on Anne's door. "Anne," he said, his voice a growl.

"Yes, Grandfather?"

"Come and prepare dinner."

Joseph brushed past Thomas, who had been keeping watch in the corridor. Anne followed, and he wondered if he heard something being mouthed or whispered behind him. The sound vanished when he turned around. The stairs were always dangerous, tall and steep and darker than the rest of the house; Joseph missed a step and stumbled. Anne's hands were suddenly under his armpits, pulling him upright. "I slipped," he muttered, brushing her off.

When they reached the ground floor, he tried to find her face. "My dear," he said.

"Yes?" she said. He heard something hard in her voice.

"I hope you know that all of this, keeping you all upstairs, it's . . . it's very painful for me. I hope you understand that I'm just trying to keep you safe."

"I understand that, Grandfather. But—"

"But?"

She paused. "But it feels like we're being punished. I don't believe we've done anything wrong."

"It may feel like a punishment but it's for your own good."

"How is this for our own good? We're stuck in our stifling rooms. We long to be together, out in the fresh air. You're treating us like prisoners."

"Anne," he said slowly. "You must understand. There are worse things than having to spend a few days inside—much worse. It's only until you girls start feeling a bit better and everything blows over. There are people in the village who wish you harm."

"I know that," she said. She spoke forcefully—she was much closer than he realised. "Do you think I don't know that?" She stopped and retreated. When she continued, her voice was quiet and low. "If no one wished us any harm we'd be happy right now. We'd be normal. None of this would have happened."

"What do you mean by that?"

She was silent for some time; he wondered if she'd left the room without him realising. He reached out and touched her face. He cupped her cheek with his hand. "What do you mean?"

"Nothing, Grandfather. Don't worry. I want what's best for my sisters, just as you do."

He let his hand drop to his side. "Good. Very good. I know I can rely on you."

Later, he helped her carry the food up to the bedrooms; he felt anger smouldering from behind each door. He put his hand up to the wood. "This won't be for long, girls," he said, but he wasn't sure if anyone heard him.

NINETEEN

TEMPERANCE WASN'T SPEAKING TO HER HUSBAND. SHE made her not-speaking known by putting herself constantly in his way—after all, what good was withholding speech if she was only to sit alone upstairs? She was always where he needed to be: at the bar, in the yard selecting casks, going to or from the latrine. When they met, she said nothing, and with each meeting he said more. By the end of the first day, he was shouting and swearing; her not-speaking had worn at him, needled him, turned him into something furious and loud. She was pleased about this.

The argument had started when John readmitted Pete Darling into the alehouse after Temperance said he wasn't to be served any more. It wasn't just about the Mansfield girls, although that was part of it; Temperance was worried about Pete, the amount he was drinking. Slurring speech, a cracked skull: she saw how it would end. He was no longer working and spent all day at the Swan or staggering along the river. He was to be married in two days, there was much for him to do—instead he drank until he could barely stand. He never seemed to go home; at the end of each long summer evening, he stumbled down to the riverbank and slept where he fell. John felt this was none of their business. "He's a loyal customer, Temp," he said.

That was when the not-speaking started.

Now it was just past breakfast, and Pete Darling sat in his usual seat at the window, watching the villagers pick their way across the almost-dry riverbed. "Temperance," he called, lifting his empty tankard. "Bring me another one. And come and talk to me while I drink it—it's been a long time since we last talked."

Temperance scowled at John. "Do as he says," John said.

She took the pint over and placed it in front of Pete. He looked up at her, the rims of his eyes poppy-red.

"Here's your drink, Pete. But I won't sit with you, because you're in no fit state to talk. Look at you—you should be ashamed of yourself."

He frowned at her. "I'm the last person on earth who should feel ashamed."

She snorted. "I see. You've got nothing at all to be ashamed of, have you?"

"That's it," he said, swaying slightly. "Exactly."

She reached for his empty tankard with a gloved hand.

"Please, Temperance, talk to me. I'm to be married this Saturday. I'm afraid."

She wavered for a moment, then pulled up a seat across from him. "What are you afraid of?"

"I'm afraid my wife will be a burden to me."

"Oh, you wretch. Of course she won't! She'll look after you, she'll keep your house. You'll be lucky to have her."

"Look after—I know what that means. That means she'll be watching every little thing I do. That means she'll make my life miserable if I stay out drinking, or if I fall asleep by the river, or if I act in any way she disapproves of." He gestured across at her and then at John. "All wives are the same."

Temperance reached up and tugged his greasy hair. "That's for being an ungrateful shit."

He caught her arm and held it tightly; with his other hand he pulled off her glove. She struggled but failed to free herself and watched, pained, as he forced her fingers into his pint of ale. "There," he murmured. "Not so bad, is it?"

She looked at him with loathing, then twisted her arm out of his grip and wiped her fingers on her skirt. "You're going to get yourself in trouble one of these days, Pete. And when that day comes, I won't do anything to help you."

The door swung open, and Richard Wildgoose wandered in, gripping his cap in his hand. Temperance stood up. "What are you doing here, Richard?" she asked. Then, seeing he was alone: "Where's Robin?"

"I came without him," he said, not looking her in the eye. "I'm here to see Pete Darling."

"Ah," Pete said, standing, slapping Richard on the shoulder. "There you are. I was wondering when I'd be seeing you again. Barmaid—bring the boy his first pint."

It worried Temperance to see the two of them together. What business had Pete Darling with young Richard? Robin wouldn't like him talking to Pete; the boys' mother wouldn't want him in the alehouse at all. But what could she do? John was eyeing her from behind the bar, where he smoked his pipe in silence. She brushed past him wordlessly and poured Richard a drink.

"Very good," Pete said as she placed it on the table. "Now, Wildgoose, what news have you got for me?"

"Well, there was one thing . . ." Richard said.

He was right on the brink of adolescence, Temperance

could see, straddling the worlds of boyhood and manhood. Things were no longer as they had been for him as a child, easy and natural. Every action he took or decision he made sent him in the direction of one or the other, boy or man; he seemed to bear this heavily. He eyed his drink for a long while before taking a sip.

"Good lad!" Pete crowed.

Temperance crossed her arms and watched them.

"What was the thing, then, Wildgoose?" Pete said, leaning towards him. "The one thing you were going to tell me?"

Richard put down the tankard, folding his hands in his lap. He nodded, as though encouraging himself to speak. "The fact is," he said, looking at his knees, "when you invited me to confide in you, I thought to myself: No. I've got a brother whom I trust very much. I don't need Pete Darling to tell me what's true and what's untrue."

Temperance peeked at Pete's face. She was pleased to see he looked put out.

"But then," Richard continued, "a curious thing happened to me. And try as I might, I can't make Robin believe me. But I saw it. With my own eyes. So now I feel I must tell someone else."

Pete observed Richard with interest. He put down his drink and wiped his mouth with the back of his hand. "What did you see?"

Richard's eyes widened. "I saw five dogs."

"No," Temperance said across the room.

"Yes," he said, turning to her. The look on his face seemed almost pleading. "I did, I swear it. Five dogs, late last night, running along the edge of the field where the men have been haymaking."

"That means nothing. There are lots of dogs in the village."

"Not like these dogs. Big, they were." He looked embarrassed. "They frightened me, if truth be told. I hid behind a hedge."

Temperance stepped forward. "You mustn't think anything of it. There are all sorts of stray dogs around. Anyway," she continued, "I heard from a friend who met Mansfield's maids waiting for the stagecoach to London—they told her the girls were confined by their grandfather after the visit from the doctor. They can't get out."

"Nonsense," Pete said. A line of sweat traversed the hard edges of his face. "Of course they can get out. That old man can't see a thing. In the dead of night, they could creep out without any trouble. They could roam the fields to their hearts' content."

"You have no proof that those dogs were the Mansfield girls. None at all."

Richard nodded, nervous. "Yes, Mistress Shirly. I know the need for proof. So I went back along the road, past Mansfield's farm, and there I saw that the candles were lit in the upstairs rooms. And, what's more, the gate was open. Wide open, it was!"

"The poor girls could have been having trouble sleeping. And Thomas might have left the gate open by mistake. That's easily explained."

Pete grinned at her. "There's a much easier explanation though, isn't there, Wildgoose? Those girls turned into dogs. We all know it. The only thing I don't know is why you're unable to admit it, Temperance. Why defend the Mansfields so much?"

She was aware of the stickiness of the ale on her fingers. "Because I believe those girls are being bullied," she said. "And if you call yourselves good Christian people, you'd be kind to them instead of spreading vicious stories."

Looking up, she saw Pete bristle. His nearness to God was a source of pride to him, she knew.

"Christ wasn't kind to the devil," he said, finishing his pint. "The devil doesn't deserve kindness."

Temperance tutted. "Those girls are not the devil, Pete Darling, and you know it."

"They might have been visited by him."

"Ah, yes, just as you were visited by an angel?"

Pete stood, his chair thumping to the floor. "You know nothing of these matters," he hissed. He lurched forward, supporting himself on Richard's shoulder. "You're too stupid to understand them."

The door swung open again, and Samuel Tubb, the schoolmaster, entered. His face was chalk-white. "Have you heard the news in the village?" he said, gesturing for Temperance to bring him a drink.

"No," Pete said. "What news?"

"The animals—"

"Dogs?"

"Animals. Rabbits, voles, pigeons, hens. Cart-loads of them—dead. In the ditches and hedgerows all around the hayfields. Killed by dogs, it looks like."

Temperance poured him a drink. She was agitated; the ale slopped over the rim.

"Lord have mercy," Pete said and staggered towards Tubb. "Dogs?" he said again.

"Yes."

"Must have been the girls. Tell him what you saw, Wildgoose. Go on, tell him."

Richard looked at Pete, and at Tubb, and then over at Temperance. She thought suddenly of the sturgeon that had been stranded in the reeds—trapped, beached, unable to escape. She shook her head; it was impossible for her to help him.

He turned back to the men. "I thought I saw some dogs late last night. Running near the fields."

"Yes," Pete said, smiling encouragingly. "But how many dogs were there?"

Temperance saw Richard swallow. "There were five."

"And then what did you see on your way home?"

Richard shifted, pulling his sleeves down to his fingertips. "I saw candles burning in the Mansfield house—"

"In the girls' bedrooms."

"Yes. And the front gate seemed to be ajar."

"There," Pete said, triumphant. "Don't you see? It was the girls. The devil changed them into dogs, and they've gone out and butchered all those animals."

Temperance tried to quieten her fluttering heart. "How many animals, Tubb? Animals are always being killed round here, you know that. It could be foxes."

Tubb observed her, a nasty smile on his lips. "Scores of them. You just go and see for yourself. No fox could have done it."

Fury swept over her. She was furious with the lot of them: with John, sitting in surly silence, sucking on his pipe; with gossiping Samuel Tubb; even young Wildgoose. But most of all she was furious with Pete, and his arrogance, and his angel, and the raging emptiness inside him. She untied her apron and flung it on the floor, and without a word to any of them she marched out into the torrid morning.

It gave her pleasure to make her way across the riverbed,

hopping—one, two, three—over the ebbing Thames, forgoing Pete's ferry for her own feet. The village was busy on the other side. In some people's faces she found a look of fear, but in others—most of them, in fact—was something hungrier, an electric excitement. She kept her head lowered and pressed along the road, past the Mansfield house, which was shut up and quiet, and down the track to the fields. A crowd had gathered there, Robin Wildgoose among them.

"Robin!" she called. "What's happening?"

"Good day, Temperance," he said, his face flushed. "I haven't been able to start work this morning. Everybody's gathered to see the dead animals."

He seemed to shrink from his own words, and his hand, which he lifted now to indicate the animals, was shaking. Temperance followed his fingers along the edge of the field. Lying on the grass, sheltered by the reaching stems of ragwort and poppies, were the carcasses of several small creatures. Limp and lifeless—some were curled as if in sleep, others folded backwards, bent, bloodied. There were rabbits, their bodies sagging like sails on a windless day. There were stoats with cold, unseeing eyes and voles and pigeons and shrews. There was even, further along, a young fallow deer, its throat torn and dappled coat covered in blood. Kites whistled overhead; again Temperance thought of the sturgeon beached on the riverbank at the beginning of this whole business. The villagers went from one creature to the next, crouching and prodding, as though observing spectacles at a fair.

"People think it was the girls," she said in a quiet voice to Robin.

He looked at her and said almost calmly: "Who?"

"Your brother has been at the Swan with Pete Darling. He told him what he saw last night—the five dogs, the candles burning at the Mansfield house, the open gate."

His face grew pinker. He wiped his forehead on his sleeve. "Richard can't have been at the Swan, not with Pete."

"I've just come from there. I heard everything he said."

"No," he said. "Richard's a boy. He doesn't go to alehouses. He wouldn't tell stories, not to Pete Darling."

"He says it's true, what he saw last night. When the village hears about it . . ." She gestured at the people flocking around the edges of the field.

"No," Robin said again, taking off his cap and running his hands through his hair. "People are reasonable. They won't jump to foolish conclusions."

Temperance bit her lip. "I fear for the girls."

Robin nodded. After a moment, he said: "Richard can't be at the alehouse. He can't be spreading these stories, not after I told him not to."

"It's Pete. He's spurring him on."

She saw, in Robin's face, rage wrestle with his usual gentleness. It was rare to see this boy become angry.

"I'm going to put a stop to it," he said.

He stalked off, abandoning the haymaking, although perhaps it didn't matter—he wasn't likely to work that day, anyhow. The field had become an attraction, and Farmer Mansfield was nowhere to be seen.

Walking back along the track to the road, Temperance passed little whispering groups returning to the village. "Dogs," she heard repeatedly. And: "Girls." *Dogs* and *girls*, over and over. Those girls are in danger, she thought.

Anxious, she brought her fingernails to her teeth and

chewed. She tasted something bitter—the ale Pete had forced on her fingers earlier. It was a new taste: much stronger than the smell that came off the casks. It tasted of the earth and of the river after a big rain. She liked the taste. Yes—it worried her that she liked the taste so much. She stopped listening to the whispered *dogs*, the whispered *girls*. She stopped thinking about the poor dead animals. She didn't hear or see or think; instead, she sucked her fingers until every last lick of ale was gone.

TWENTY

THE NIGHT BEFORE HIS WEDDING, PETE DREAMED OF RAIN. Thunderous clouds erupting into showers, thick droplets hitting the river, water streaming off leaves and over muddied banks—he saw it all as he slept, and he felt soothed. He hoped, when he woke, that this dream might be a portent and his wedding would bring the dry weather to an end, but when dawn broke and he stepped outside, he saw that it would be another day of scorching heat. He felt encaged by it, the Eden of his beloved countryside made menacing and barren. The birds were silent, but the crickets shrieked.

If there'd be no rain, he hoped that God might send him some other sign, a blessing for his marriage, and throughout his breakfast he kept watch in case there should be a visitation. While he waited for the visitation, he drank. He thought about many things as he sat there, but his future wife was not one of them. For some reason, it seemed important not to think about her this morning, to think instead about angels and the unnatural drought—anything but Agnes Bullock.

He felt like a fish caught in the mouth of a moving whale; he was subject to currents outside his control. No power on earth could extract him now, and he could do nothing but allow himself to be carried. By the end of the day, this would all be over. He and his bride would be conveyed to bed by tipsy villagers, who'd strip them of their stockings and sing outside their window, just as Pete had frequently done to other newlyweds before. Weddings were a time for revelries and games, all of which Pete usually enjoyed, but today was his own wedding, and he found he didn't have the stomach for festivity. It seemed as if his life was ending.

He couldn't sit like this until mid-morning, when he was due to be at the church. He would go mad with waiting, so he stood and paced around his cottage and finished another few cups of ale and then, feeling unsteady, made his way down to the river for some fresh air. This stretch of riverbank was always where he had been happiest. It had nothing to do with the angel, for he'd felt it since boyhood, long before the visitation ever happened; it was to do with the way the willow trailed its branches into the water, and the swans which nested here every May, and also to do with his father, but he wasn't sure exactly why. He didn't miss his father, who had been rude and rageful, but he missed the idea of him, and sometimes, standing by the Thames, the idea of his father returned to him very strongly. He hoped to feel this fatherly idea today and walked along the bank to seek it out, but the air was hot and empty, and the riverbed was dry. He felt very alone.

It was here, just here, beside this clump of bulrushes, that he had first seen the Mansfield sisters turn into dogs, and he shivered a little as he passed the spot. They were a blight on the face of the village, and he was glad to hear that they'd been confined. He wanted no sign of them on his wedding day. True, his future father-in-law had invited Joseph Mansfield to the celebration, but Pete didn't mind the old man so much—it was the girls he hated, and God had made it so they couldn't attend.

He wasn't sure what would happen to the girls. Some said that Mansfield was looking to move, to make a fresh start where he and his granddaughters weren't known. Others said he'd agreed at last to have the vicar come and exorcise them. At the alehouse, a story had gone round that the old man had blocked in the girls' bedrooms because he was afraid of being eaten by them in his sleep. Pete didn't blame him, if this were true. He would never admit it aloud—it demeaned him even to think it—but the girls frightened him to death. They had done so even before they were dogs.

The heat and the ale were working on his body; he felt breathless and found for himself a hillock of dry moss to sit on. Here the tall teasels, once purple, now brown, whispered around him, and he rested on his elbows and tried to still the spinning landscape. He knew in his bones that he was blessed, but he longed for some extra sign today. The girls were confined, and that was good, but he wanted more. He wanted to know for certain that God was smiling down on him.

Just as he was thinking this, his gaze caught on a flash of white across the river, and he fumbled to his feet. Was it a heron? He squinted at the far bank, his eyes beginning to stream. The flash of white grew brighter and rippled in a way no heron ever had. Could it be—? He barely dared to hope, but something in his chest seemed to confirm it. He took another step, toeing the edge of the bank. Bliss overcame him. He burst into tears, and through the blur he saw the angel, the same one as before, smiling across at him. A curious warmth coursed through him, an ecstasy. He sank to his knees and smiled at the angel, and the angel looked kindly at him, and he knew that he was blessed.

When he woke (for suddenly, strangely, he found he was asleep), he saw that the bank was empty again, but it didn't matter. The angel had visited, and this confirmed for Pete that he'd been right about everything. He was right about the Mansfield girls, and he was right to get married. He walked with purpose along the withered path towards the church.

The ground seemed to hiss with the heat—by now the sun was high—and the dry grass flattened easily underfoot. Everything shimmered. Above the hissing another note sounded, something thin and uneasy: a moan. Another moan joined it. And another. A chorus of moans reached him from the village, and he felt instantly sober as he hurried up to the road. Strands of hay danced on the deserted lane as he searched for the source of the noise. Who was crying? The sounds seemed to come from almost every direction, and now he could hear another noise too, a deep, desperate scratching, claws digging into wood.

He saw Martha Heathcote—gossip-monger, baker's wife—sweeping her doorstep. "Martha," he called, his voice a little choked. "What's happening?"

She stopped sweeping and leaned on her broom, observing him. "Pete Darling," she said with a smile. "Aren't you getting married this morning?"

"I am, Martha," he said. "But what's all this noise?"

He gestured, but there was nothing to point to. The sound was everywhere. It filled the air, the earth, the inside of his own head.

"Oh," she said, resuming her sweeping. "That's the dogs."

"The dogs?"

"Yes. After all those animals were killed down by the hayfields, it was decided that the dogs should be locked up. All of them, every dog in the village. Until we discover which one of them did it."

"But, Martha," he said, gaping. "You know as well as I do—we all know—that it was those girls who did it. It was no dog."

She didn't look up. "They say that's impossible."

"But we know it's possible. We've seen them."

"Let them test the idea, for all I care. Something unholy is bound to happen, and then we'll know for certain it wasn't the dogs."

"It won't happen today."

She frowned at him and stopped sweeping. "Hmm?"

"Nothing unholy will happen today. I'm getting married today. God won't allow any unholiness."

Her face puckered with laughter. "If you say so, Pete."

"He won't allow it," he repeated, petulant.

Martha stopped laughing, resting her gaze on him for a moment longer, then went inside, and Pete was alone once more, listening to the moaning, the sniffing, the scratching. It sounded, he thought, walking slowly through the village, like the inside of a madman's mind, tormenting and loud. The sun beat down on him, and the dust caught in his throat and made him cough. He thought about the angel and resolved not to be troubled by the noises or the heat. He would forge a path through the wilderness and come out untouched on the other side. Nothing could overcome him: no power of evil, no woman or girl or wife. Not even the devil himself could do it, for Pete was good and strong and would prevail over any enemy. That was the vow he voiced to himself as he made his way to be married.

TWENTY-ONE

Despite their new roles as jailer and prisoner, Joseph and Anne continued their usual morning ritual, wherein she bathed his eyes and fetched his beer, and he asked her questions about how she and her sisters were faring. The words they exchanged remained the same: dull back-and-forths about the things Anne required for the household, Joseph's thoughts on farm matters, Hester's fits of bad temper, Grace's earaches. In this, nothing had changed. But everything else had shifted, inflected with Anne's fury and Joseph's sadness and a thousand other unspoken things. He could feel it in the air, and in the way Anne touched his face. She told him the girls were doing fine, but her breath, her hands, said otherwise. It was there Joseph heard the heartbreaking truth: that his granddaughters were growing to hate him.

Yet what could he do? He was only trying to protect them. He rarely went into the village any more, but he understood—from whispers overheard in the field during haymaking and Mildmay's awkward reports—that the villagers hadn't forgotten how they felt about the girls, and that the fear they had of them was only growing in their absence.

"My child," he said, when Anne had finished wiping his cheeks, "there's something I need to discuss with you."

He heard her balling the linen in her lap. "What is it, Grandfather?"

He breathed out deeply and his shoulders sagged. "I believe the time will soon come when we'll have to leave this farmhouse and find another home."

"No!" she said. "We can never do that."

"I think we must. You and your sisters can't remain inside forever."

"We won't have to. Things will change very soon."

"I thought so too, my dear. I thought the villagers would move on to other things. But I believe they haven't, that they might never do so."

Her breath was quick. "But this is our home. This is where we lived with our grandmother, where our father grew up."

"I know."

"And for us to have to leave, to be bullied out of Little Nettlebed . . . No," she said, her voice becoming low. "We won't do it."

"Don't you want your freedom, child?"

She was quiet for a moment, and then she spoke. "Wherever we go, however we behave, there'll always be something to drive us inside. That's where people want us to be. That was our mistake, right at the start of this whole business . . ." She grew silent again, and he heard her lift her hand to her face. "We went out when we weren't supposed to, we were too free, and this—all of this—is our punishment. It has nothing to do with the idea of us becoming dogs, and everything to do with the fact of us being girls."

His shoulders sagged still further.

"I refuse to run away," she continued. "This is our home. Our farm, our livelihood. We can't leave this place. You mustn't make us."

Joseph wished he had her courage. He felt cowardly and remote, cut off from his granddaughters. It was no longer simply that he had locked them in; he sensed that the girls had also shut him out. He wanted to find them again, to see Anne clearly, to draw strength from her face. He pushed himself to his feet. "Come," he said. "We're going outside."

The heat, which hit him the moment he stepped out of the house, was so heavy he felt as though he might fall. Anne caught his arm, and they stood like that for a while, holding each other in the yard. At length, he glanced down and found her upturned face, eyes closed against the sun. He believed he could see more than ever, misted, blurring images sharpening in the bright summer light. He watched as she basked in the warmth, her mouth remembering its way into a smile. Her grip on his arm tightened. He pulled away.

"I'm sorry I've confined you to the house, Anne," he said. "I thought it was best. I wanted you all to rest, as the doctor said. I didn't want people prying, trying to catch a glimpse of you."

She breathed out and opened her eyes. "Please—it's such a beautiful day. Can't the others come out into the garden, just for a little while?"

Her flushed, hopeful look swam into focus. "I don't know, my dear. I'm not—"

"Please, Grandfather. Everyone in the village will be up at the church for Pete Darling's wedding. No one will see us."

"Yes," he said slowly. "That's true."

"We'll be inside by the time you get back. Long before then."

He paused. "Very well. But no one must see you. Stay in the

orchard, away from the wall. No one is to go beyond the gate. And after he's escorted me to the church, I'll ask Mildmay to come back to be with you."

"Of course," she said. "Thank you so much."

She kissed him then, and—hearing the news over breakfast—the others all took turns in kissing him too: five soft kisses on his sorry cheek.

"I'm going now, girls," he said when they'd finished eating. "Please be careful."

Walking with Mildmay out of the gate and up the lane, Joseph felt a growing sense of foreboding. He tried to ignore it; it was probably just the prospect of being among the other villagers. He hadn't wanted to attend Pete's wedding but believed he should, to quell the stories he knew would be going around in his absence. He wouldn't stay for the celebrations afterwards. Pete Darling wasn't someone he had any desire to celebrate.

The feeling grew as they passed along the high road. The air seemed to ring with the sound of dogs, whining and pawing behind closed doors. Joseph tried to keep up a brisk pace. He felt watched, his skin prickling with the stares of unseen eyes.

"We're here," Mildmay murmured. "Shall I take you to your pew?"

"No," Joseph said, patting his hand. "I can find it. Go back to the house and keep an eye on the girls. If there's any trouble, take them inside and come and get me. Understood?"

"Yes, sir."

He was sorry when Mildmay had gone and he was left alone outside the church. He was uneasy, the feeling of foreboding swelling in his chest. The bell that sounded in the tower made him tremble; it wasn't a joyful noise. He heard chattering but could see no faces. He felt unmoored. This church, this wedding, was no place for him; he yearned to be back at home. But no, these were foolish thoughts—he belonged here just as much as anyone. His wife was buried here, and his beloved son, and the mother of his granddaughters. It gladdened him to think of them. He might be half-blind and hated by his neighbours, but he had known the love of a good family, and that was something to be bolstered by. He walked towards the door, chin raised, eyes fixed to the invisible heavens.

The babbling voices hushed when he walked in. It was cooler in the church than it had been outside, and he was struck by the scent of sweet sedge rising from the floor where it had been scattered and crushed by people's feet. Light was scarce, and he couldn't see far, feeling his way to his pew with an outstretched hand. The air was thick with whispers.

At last, silence descended, and Joseph heard the vicar rustle to the pulpit, where he spoke lengthily and dully on the duty of marriage. Joseph tried to concentrate, but he was aware that he was being observed, and every so often he thought he heard muttering behind him. He kept his head up and didn't flinch, even when he heard the word *dogs* hissed unmistakably and a titter spread through the congregation. The service would be over soon, and he could go home.

Now the bride was being presented to Pete Darling, and Joseph could hear their hands meeting. This seemed to distract the congregation, which fidgeted appreciatively as it waited for Pete to give Agnes Bullock his ring. Nearly there, Joseph thought. He wasn't sure why he longed to leave with such urgency—it was something to do with the terrible tightness in his chest, and also with his granddaughters. He wished he hadn't agreed to Anne's suggestion that they spend some time in the garden; he wished they were confined to their rooms, as they had been before. But what trouble could they get into, really? The villagers were all here, and, anyway, Mildmay would be with them, keeping watch. He felt he could trust Mildmay. The boy cared about his work.

The ring was given, and a ripple passed over the crowd. Joseph had one tense hand on the pew in front of him, preparing to stand. It was almost time. Almost—

A sound carried through the church. It was so strange, so surprising, that it took Joseph a moment to comprehend what he was hearing. He noticed other things first. A change in the air. What had been cool became bleakly cold. The gleeful, chattering voices were silenced—not in a soft, subsiding way, but sharply, suddenly, like a candle blown out with one quick breath. He heard people turning to look at the door. He felt his hands begin to shake. It was as though they could see what he could not. He wasn't a praying man, but a prayer formed in his mind, unsummoned. *Please*, he thought, *protect my granddaughters*.

Now Joseph understood what he was hearing, understood that everyone in the church was responding to a sound from outside. Something—*someone*—was barking. The sound had a mocking note. He could picture it coming from the mouths of dogs, or jackdaws, or demons. Not girls, though. Not lovely, gentle girls, waiting in a garden at home. This sound was far too wild, too violent; no girl could contain it. But so much had surprised Joseph this summer. Much as he feared the idea, much as it filled him with dread, he knew it was possible that the barking sound was being made by his own granddaughters. The thought gripped him with panic. He couldn't stay here. The congregation was growing restless. He pushed himself to his feet and felt his way down the aisle.

Along the way, his foot met with something—a leg, was

it, or a hassock?—and he stumbled, groping for support. He found the edge of a pew and leaned on it, trying to steady his shaking hands. He felt someone beside him—someone come to help him, perhaps. But no—the person, a man, pushed past him down the aisle, and Joseph let out a sob of frustration. He wanted to be outside, in a place of brightness, far away from the dark, cold church. He feared he would be trapped there forever.

People were shoving past him, and he allowed himself to be taken with the crowd to the door. The barking had stopped, but still no one spoke above a murmur. Joseph felt as though he was being carried on the replenished river, listening to a babbling current around him. It spat him out in the churchyard, and he staggered, blinking, adjusting to the daylight.

"Where's Pete?" someone shouted.

"He must have gone after them," someone else said.

"After who?" said another voice. "We didn't see who it was."

"Don't be a fool," someone close to Joseph said. "We know very well."

Somebody jostled him. Squinting, he found himself face-to-face with Humphrey Bullock and his daughter, her face blotched, her hands wrestling with the ribbons on her dress. Bullock seemed to be wearing a wig made from his own daughter's hair: youthful, yellow wisps framed his furious face. Joseph stepped backwards, his arms outstretched as though in surrender. He sought the dark bank of yew trees at the edge of the churchyard and waited there, his breath loud, his hands still trembling.

"They're probably down by the river," a man said, walking away, and the other voices snaked after him, leaving Joseph alone in the shadows.

He wished he could seek guidance from his family, buried

in the earth a few yards away, but he felt nothing from them now: they were only bones. *Please*, he thought again, clutching his hands to his chest, *protect my granddaughters*. But his prayer was met with silence, and the fear inside him wasn't subdued. Picking his way around hazy headstones, hurrying back down the road, he arrived at a decision. He and the girls must pack their things and have Mildmay prepare the horses. The time had come for them to flee.

TWENTY-TWO

Like all the others, Robin watched agog as Pete marched out of his wedding ceremony to pursue the sound of barking. He and Richard left the church with the surging crowd and followed the stream of people to the river.

"Robin," Richard said, "do you think it was—"

"I don't know, Dickie," he said sharply. "None of us know. Let's just wait and see."

He would never admit it to Richard, but he felt frightened. It was like the night of badger-baiting at the alehouse. There was a hunger in the air, a lust, which would only end in violence; he'd seen it so often before. Perhaps they could peel off now, he and Richard—follow the lane up to their cottage and be no part of it. But they were hemmed in by the crowd, and Richard was grinning, carried away with the general hysteria. They would have to continue. They had no choice but to see how these events turned out.

People gathered in scattered groups on the bank, watching, not wanting to dirty their best clothes in the ebbing brown water. Robin squeezed through them, Richard close behind him, and together they walked through the shallow river. A figure was standing on the far side—Pete, it looked like—cradling his arm. "I've been bitten," he said, not loudly, not furiously, but soft as a snake moving through grass. "Here, on my hand."

Robin saw Pete's hand wrapped in his jacket, and then saw bright drops of blood on his shirt where he'd pressed his hand to his chest. He froze. "Who bit you?" he said, forcing out the words which stuck dryly in his throat.

"You know who it was," Pete said.

"No," Robin said, shaking his head. "I don't."

"It was the eldest Mansfield sister. She bit me."

They were silent, fathoming it. The sweat slipped down Robin's forehead into his stinging eyes.

"What happened?" someone called from the other side.

Robin saw Pete look over at Richard, who nodded. "Pete Darling's been bitten," Richard shouted, his face pale. "By Anne Mansfield."

Robin heard the gasp from the far bank carry across the river like a breeze.

"Let's see it, the bite," he said, stepping towards Pete.

Pete gave him an ugly look. "You don't believe me."

"Of course I do."

He unwrapped his hand. The skin had been punctured in a neat row, little rubies of blood glistening from each nick. "She's got sharp teeth," Pete said.

"Was it a girl, or was it a dog?"

Pete pulled his hand back and swaddled it in his jacket once more. "Both. It was Anne Mansfield."

"But did she look to you like a dog this time? Or was she still a girl?"

"I—" He frowned. "She was a dog. But I saw her turn back into a girl. It happened before my eyes."

"Could it have been one of the dogs that's been locked up all day? Maybe it was angry. Maybe it managed to break free and bit you."

"No," Pete said, shaking his head. "Definitely not. It was the girl, I swear it."

Robin saw in Richard's face a panicked look. He had believed what Pete had said; he had even shouted it across the river.

"Let's go," someone called from the other bank. "Let's get the girls. Where did you see them go, Pete?"

Pete frowned harder. "I didn't see. My hand . . . I was trying to stop the bleeding."

Samuel Tubb stepped forward. "We'll go up to the Mansfields' house," he called. "You three head down the river and see if you can find them there. We'll meet back at the Swan."

Pete nodded and gestured for them to go. "Are you coming?" he said to Robin and Richard, before starting down the path.

Robin looked at Richard, who didn't meet his eye, slinking off behind Pete. Breathless, he went after them. It must have been approaching noon; the sun hung directly above them, and the ground grew riven like bark, and Robin saw stranded fish leap and gasp. A rabbit ran in circles ahead. Beneath their crisp footsteps, Robin heard something—Pete muttering under his breath. Robin quickened his pace, listening. "Going to make them suffer," Pete was saying. "Going to make them wish they were dead. Worse than dead—"

Robin fell back, disturbed. What would happen when they discovered the girls? He would rather walk through this arid meadow forever than find out. The price they'd be made to pay for Pete's wounded pride was a heavy one.

"Look," Richard said, pointing.

Sitting on the bank ahead, shaded by a large weeping willow, were five black-clad figures. They were arranged in a languid circle, leaning on one another's shoulders, looking palely out over the dead river. One of them was eating an apple.

"Hey," Richard shouted. "It's them!"

With a boyish burst of energy, he broke into a run, then seemed to remember where he was and slowed to keep abreast with Pete. Robin saw something twitch in Pete's face and his bloodshot eyes narrow. He strode up to them, and Robin followed, fearful. He saw that the girls' mourning dresses were powdered with dust, and that the youngest, Mary, had a line of mud on her cheek. He saw the dark, sleepless circles around their eyes, and their unsunned skin, and their pouting mouths. He saw that he'd been wrong: there weren't just five of them. Thomas Mildmay was there too, next to Anne, and he got to his feet now, curls falling into his flushing face.

"What do you want?" Thomas said.

Pete gave an enraged croak and threw his bloodied jacket on the ground. "I want to know why these girls, these . . . *bitches*, seem intent on ruining my wedding day, and"—he gestured at his hand—"and, and why they *bit* me, and why they've set about plaguing me all summer." He pulled himself to his full height and looked down at Thomas. "I'm here to take them back to the village."

Thomas shook his head, and his flush grew deeper. He cradled his fist in a cupped hand. "How dare you speak about them like that?" he said. "They've done none of the things you've accused them of. They've done nothing today but sit in their garden and now, because they wished to see the dried-up river, walk a little along the path. I've attended to them all morning. There has been no biting. No ruining of weddings."

Richard gave Pete a nervous look, then flashed a glance at Robin. Pete stepped closer to Thomas and lowered his voice. "I know what I saw, Mildmay. I've been bitten, look. That girl"—he jabbed a finger at Anne—"she bit me."

Anne stood, the colour fierce in her cheeks. "You're lying," she said.

The other girls stood too, Grace holding Mary's hand, Elizabeth blinking back tears. Hester stepped forward to stand beside Thomas. Robin wished that the wasted ground would rupture, or that the river would return in a great, rushing flood, or that the heavens would open and envelop them in cascading rain. He longed not to be there, in the crackling heat. He longed to be far away—far from Pete, who seethed with anger, and Thomas, deliriously faithful to the girls, and Richard, biting his lip behind Robin, and the Mansfield sisters, who he feared might actually turn into dogs and eat Pete Darling before his very eyes. He wanted no part in the rage which ringed them all together. It horrified him; it made him sick.

"Leave them," Thomas said. "Go back to your wedding celebrations. The young ladies have done nothing wrong."

Pete leaned forward, bumping his chest into Thomas's shoulder. "No," he said. "They're coming with me."

Thomas pushed Pete away. "They will not go with you."

Robin heard a beating, a pulsing, his heart working loudly in his body.

"Richard," Pete said over his shoulder, "hold back the girls."

Richard shot Robin a strangled look. Robin shook his head, but Richard's expression deadened, and he walked with his chin lifted across to the sisters. He didn't touch them but outstretched his hands to create a barrier. Hester scoffed.

"The girls are coming with me," Pete said again, drawing up his shirt sleeves. The bite on his arm was beginning to crust. "It's God's will. They must be punished."

Everything had seemed very slow, hampered by the heat, but now, without warning, things happened like lightning. Thomas pulled back his balled fist and punched Pete in the face. Pete reeled, then brought both hands to Thomas's throat, cursing. Thomas struck him in the stomach and kicked him, wriggling free from his hold. Robin watched. The girls had started shouting, and one of them, Hester, wrestled with Richard to reach the men. Robin saw something glinting in the sunlight: a knife, the knife Hester had been using to cut her apple, which she now pointed at Richard. Robin watched stupidly as Richard twisted the knife from the girl's grip, holding it high out of her reach.

Thomas spat and swung his fist at Pete's face. Pete, jumping away, gave a small, warbling cry. Robin watched as he seemed to summon strength—he looked at Thomas for a long time, very still, then launched at him again. He was again at Thomas's throat, his broad, callused hands wrapped around his neck. Thomas grew pink, unable to speak. He no longer fought. He dropped to his knees, dust rising from the ground around him. The girls were crying; one of them pushed Richard forward. "Do something," they hissed. "Thomas is going to die."

Robin saw Richard hunch. He saw his face become furrowed as it always did when he was trying not to cry. He saw him look down at the knife, then over at him. He saw Richard step towards the men. Gasping, choking for air, Robin rushed forward and took the knife from his brother.

It was warm. It jumped in his quivering hand.

He plunged it into Pete's back. It went easily, like slicing into soft dough. He pulled it out and stabbed once more, wondering again at the ease, and then a third time. He noticed, as though in a dream, patterns spreading on Pete's shirt: his lifeblood flowering hotly. Pete released his grip from Thomas's throat and staggered around to face Robin.

"What have you done, Wildgoose?" he said, veins swelling in his neck.

"I—"

His mouth was dry, full of dust. He dropped the knife; it clattered on the hard ground. Tears fell swiftly down his cheeks. They were all looking at him. Their eyes wouldn't release him. He felt trapped and also very small.

"I don't . . ." he gasped. "I'm sorry."

"Sorry!" Pete lurched towards him. "You've murdered me."

"No," Robin said, a whimper. "I didn't mean to."

"Me," Pete said, his face becoming wan. "It shouldn't be . . ."

Robin saw Hester through the blur. She took his hand; her palm was hot.

Pete sank to his knees. "It wasn't . . ." he said. He reached over and touched Robin's leg. His voice was faint. "The angel, where is he?"

His bloodshot eyes were wide and staring. Robin thought he might faint.

"I'm dying," Pete said. "God wouldn't desert me like this."

"There is no angel," Hester said furiously.

"Hester!" Elizabeth said, wiping away tears.

"What? This man deserves nothing. He wanted to kill us."

"He's dying, Hester."

They looked at him.

"I'm glad," Hester said, and kicked a stone.

Now Pete was on his back, blood pooling like wings around him. The brilliant sky settled in his unblinking eyes.

"He's dead," Anne said, her voice trembling.

Richard let out a sob, and silence descended.

TWENTY-THREE

THOMAS TOUCHED HIS THROAT. IT WAS BRUISED, AND HE found it painful to swallow. He felt unsteady, flickering specks of white and grey dancing in front of his eyes. Through the haze, he'd seen Pete's face change. Now it was mask-like: lifeless and unmoving, frozen in its final bewildered state.

Pete was dead. Thomas looked up at Anne, and Robin and Richard Wildgoose, and the other girls. Anne frowned for a long time at the body, while Elizabeth moved Mary and Grace away, guiding their eyes to a row of ducks waddling across the wide rock riverbed.

"What have I done?" Robin said in a hoarse whisper.

Thomas saw that he wasn't well. He was green and sweating, his lip shaking.

"Nothing," Hester said, picking the knife up from the ground and cleaning it on her dress. It left a slick purple mark. "We were all in danger. You saved us."

Thomas nodded and stepped forward to pat the boy on the back. "You saved my life. Don't dwell on it any more. If it hadn't been you, any one of us could have done it. He was crazy, blood-hungry—we wouldn't have made it out alive otherwise."

Robin nodded, his mouth downcast. Anne stepped towards him and kissed him lightly on the cheek. "Thank you," she said. "That man was a monster."

Robin winced. He looked over at his brother. Thomas saw something pass between them, something wordless and vast.

"We should do something with the body," he said, squinting at the kites circling in the sky. "It'll rot or be eaten if we leave it lying here."

It was awful, the shift from *he* to *it*. Moments ago, this thing, this lump of wasted flesh, had been a man.

Anne gave him a hard look. "We can't do anything with it," she said. "We need to leave before anyone sees us."

From the bank, Mary made a sound—not speech, exactly—and Elizabeth clutched her shoulder. Thomas, seeing Robin's stare, recalled hearing how he had carefully buried each of his hens after they had been slaughtered; *as though they were deserving of peace*, the lad who told him had scoffed.

"Let's go," Grace said quietly. "Before we're found."

They were right: the body would have to be left. It was too large for them to carry; there was no river to sling it into. No one had seen what they'd done. They could go, enclose themselves in the house, stay forever unfound. In that moment, Thomas almost believed it.

Robin was still crying. "I can't—" he said, his shoulders lifting with soft hiccoughing sobs. "I need—"

Thomas saw Anne approach Robin and take both his hands. Her face, so often indecipherable, was easy to read in that moment; it shone. "Breathe deeply, Robin," she said. "In and out—there you go. You mustn't be troubled. You've done something very brave today. We all owe you a great debt."

Robin shook his head and pulled away his hands. "I've

become them," he said, tears swimming around his nose and gathering in his mouth. "Don't you see? I've become them. I didn't think twice."

"Who?" Anne said. "Who have you become?"

Robin's face was the picture of fear. He looked at her, horrified. "Them," he said, and gestured outwards, over the river, the village and the fields, towards the world beyond.

They followed his finger—his juddering, outstretched finger, its bitten-down nail—and Thomas heard a sigh whisper through the group. He looked around and saw all the girls staring at the spot indicated by Robin, their faces intent, as though they had found in the wooded vista something familiar and frightening. They knew what he meant by *them*.

Elizabeth stepped forward. "You are Robin Wildgoose. Nobody else. Nothing will ever change that."

Robin folded his arms across himself, hunching his shoulders up to his ears. Now it was Richard's turn to step forward. Thomas saw the boy swallow and tuck his hair behind his ears several times. He faced Robin and drew a breath. "Pete Darling was a bad man," he said. "I shouldn't have done what he said. I was just trying . . . I didn't want . . ." He stopped.

Robin looked for a long time at his brother, then reached forward and squeezed his arm. "You have nothing to regret, Dickie."

A kite shrieked overhead. Thomas remembered where he was; for a moment he had been far away, thinking of his own brothers. "We should go," he said, and Anne nodded.

Elizabeth put her arms around Mary and Grace's shoulders, and Hester linked hers through Robin's. Thomas gave Pete's body a final look. The expression on the dead man's face disturbed him, his eyes sightless, his mouth slackened and wide. He touched his tender throat once more and turned away, following the others up the path. They walked slowly, as though their feet understood that haste was hopeless. Thomas glanced at Anne. He wanted to reassure her somehow, to let her know that everything would be fine: she was under his protection. But something knotted in his stomach, stopping him from doing so. Did she know, as he did, that they were bound to get caught? It was Pete Darling's wedding day; he would be missed, followed, found. The village was small, the girls already mistrusted. They only had a short time before they were discovered.

He looked up at the sky and closed his eyes for a moment, the sun hot on his skin. He knew what was ahead, but he couldn't help the feeling of contentment—joy, even—spreading over him. He was happy. He was here with Anne, and he was happy. Perhaps all the happier because he knew the feeling couldn't last. It was a blooming flower at the height of summer: its time was now. Soon, it would wilt and shed and die, but for a brief moment it was beautiful.

They saw the villagers before they heard them. The flash of bright jackets and ribboned dresses, the flushed and angry faces. They were up ahead, across the river, but Thomas soon saw them trickle over, lifting their skirts from the dirt and the stream of muddied water. Soon, their clamour reached him. They were calling the girls' names. *Anne, Elizabeth, Hester, Grace, Mary*—over and over, like a prayer or a spell. *Anne, Elizabeth, Hester, Grace, Mary.* Thomas saw, almost as though they'd been touched, each of the girls flinch when she heard her own name. They stopped walking and looked at each other with urgent, fearful expressions. Robin had begun to cry again.

The crowd was now up ahead, approaching fast, and the

sisters, the Wildgoose boys, and Thomas all turned inwards to face each other, forming a huddled circle. "Should we run?" Hester asked.

Anne shook her head. "We can't run."

Robin gasped. "What should we do?"

Thomas looked at Anne. "We can't do anything."

She nodded, her eyes on his face.

Now, someone behind them screamed, and they all turned. "Look," the voice said shrilly. "It's Pete."

They'd seen him lying on the grass. "He's covered in blood," another voice said.

"Murderers!" someone shouted. "Those girls are murderers."

Sobs wracked Robin's body. Thomas closed his eyes and tried to regain the feeling of joy, the warm sun on his skin. No—it was gone, perhaps forever. He opened his eyes and saw Samuel Tubb and John Shirly at the head of the approaching crowd.

"What have you done?" Tubb said to Anne, stopping a few yards away from her as though afraid to come nearer. "You've killed an innocent man."

Anne lifted her chin and was about to speak when Robin stepped forward. "It wasn't Miss Mansfield," he said, clenching his fists to stop them shaking. "It wasn't any of the girls."

Thomas's heart began to gallop. People pressed in behind Tubb and Shirly: Humphrey Bullock, his face red with heat and rage, and Agnes, whose streaming nose was buried in her sleeve, and several others whom Thomas knew, or had once known—they seemed so foreign to him now. He saw Robin draw breath to speak, and saw Richard freeze with fear, and saw the girls close their eyes. He summoned his courage and stepped forward.

"It wasn't any of the girls," Thomas repeated, his voice a croak. "It was me. I killed Pete Darling."

A gasp of outrage passed through the crowd. Anne looked over at him, and he saw for the first time the full extent of her feeling for him.

"No," someone shouted. "It was the girls. The devil has possessed them."

"It was me," Thomas said again.

"Why?" John Shirly called. "Why did you kill him?"

This required no thought, no fabrication at all. "I love Anne Mansfield," he said. "And I knew Pete Darling wouldn't rest until he'd ruined her. I couldn't let that happen."

Thomas had heard once about a machine devised by a man in Italy to see the stars. It was long and thin and acted like an ingenious eye: it saw far into the distance, discovering wonders in the heavens. Nothing could hide from it. Now, Thomas felt as though this probing eye had passed from the Mansfield sisters to him. He was caught in its unblinking gaze, and he couldn't escape. The others seemed to melt away, fading from the villagers' sight. Their distrust of the girls was temporarily forgotten.

"Grab him," Humphrey Bullock said, and Tubb stepped forward.

Robin looked at Thomas, panicked, but Thomas did nothing. He allowed the men to tie his hands behind his back with ribbon. He didn't struggle when they pressed him to walk. He tried not to look at the girls' faces.

He felt calm as they prodded him across the river. Half-submerged in the shallow water were gasping loaches, and spent mussels, and crusting weeds; he stepped over them confidently—triumphantly, almost. More villagers joined on the far side. They looked at him with loathing, but it didn't matter. On the high road, the crowd jostled and surged around him. He smelled hay and dust and sweat and felt hard hands on his back. "You'll hang for this, Mildmay," someone said.

It was true. The moment he confessed to the crime he hadn't done, he realised it. But he didn't regret what had happened, and he wasn't afraid. The sisters were safe, he said to himself. Nothing else mattered to him now.

TWENTY-FOUR

Temperance had not gone to Pete Darling's wedding. She was still angry with him—about the Mansfield girls, and about him forcing her fingers into the ale. She'd been having peculiar dreams since then: dreams in which she drank from amber fountains, in which she sang and swayed as the men in the Swan so often sang and swayed. She awoke from these dreams disturbed. She had no wish to be as her father was, his precious life wasted. She was too busy for that, too happy. But standing in the empty alehouse, listening to the voices of the villagers gathering for Pete's wedding, she wondered if she wasn't too busy, or too happy, at all.

That morning, she danced a curious dance around a cask of ale behind the bar. It was as though she was drawn to it; she found herself near it, even when her tasks took her elsewhere. At first, she kept away on purpose. She averted her eyes and turned her back and refused to let her mind wander towards it. Soon, she allowed herself a glimpse, and then a lingering look. Next, she passed her fingers over the barrel and brought them to her nose, but it wasn't enough. She pressed her face into her hands, burying herself in the smell of bitter hops. For a moment, she caught it: that delicious, heady flavour, fading so swiftly. It was a flame, a shadow, impossible to pin down.

She almost convinced herself that this would be sufficient, the smell of the ale on her fingers. She assured herself that she wasn't in any danger—though just as she was thinking this, without really knowing what she was doing, she pulled a tankard down from the shelf. She hadn't actually done anything yet; it was merely a flirtation. But the ale knew otherwise. It seemed to summon her. At last she realised, with a fluttering feeling in her chest, that she was no match for it.

It was a relief, in a way, to submit to it. To acknowledge to herself that she was weak and the drink was strong. Why did she think she could withstand it, when so many others could not? She loved her father, and now she understood him. It felt binding to share his vice.

She began to pour, marvelling at the ale's tawny colour as it swilled into her cup, the scent, the foaming head. Her mouth was dry, and she brought the drink to her lips. Oh, she thought, here was relief after heat and work. Here was happiness. Here was peace. The ale moved over her body quickly, filling her throat, lightening her limbs, and tickling her skin. She was a stray lamb which had been found, a lost object restored. She was home. Yes, this cup was a home to her, the best home she'd ever had, the one that wanted her the most. She drank deeply. The drink didn't lose its wonder; the flavours only grew richer as she reached its dregs, the wisdom it imparted all the more profound.

She poured herself a second pint, thinking of Pete Darling. Perhaps she didn't dislike Pete so much. Recently, she'd thought him arrogant and deluded, but something about him had always appealed to her. His oddness, maybe. His simplicity.

And now she wondered if he wasn't so very arrogant after all. He had known something that she had not: the transcendent taste of drink, the freedom and refreshment it offered. He had given it to her. She was converted. The least she could do was to congratulate him on his wedding day.

She wiped the back of her hand over her mouth and tried to untie her apron. She tugged at it for a while, but the knot wouldn't come undone. It didn't matter. She staggered to the door and down to the river, which she was surprised to find had disappeared. Of course—the heat, the rainless days. But where was Pete? Yes, she remembered now. He was getting married, and that was why she was going into the village.

She picked her way across the river, staring for a long time at the debris that lined the rocky bed. She found mussel shells, blackened and grooved, and small, rotting bodies. They fascinated her, and she crouched to see them, her apron dragging in the dirty water. There had been an entire teeming world here, before the drought had come. There had been life, and now there was nothing. Some of the shells were round and purple, others silver and thin. One of them she found herself particularly drawn to: a clam-shell, dark-edged and narrow. She lifted it carefully, testing the razor edges. A drop of glowing blood appeared on the tip of her finger. She straightened up and put the shell in her apron pocket, sucking on her finger, before continuing on her way.

Forging through the dry grass on the other side, she saw that there were people milling around on the road up ahead. The ceremony must be over, but where was the drinking and the merriment? The faces that turned towards her as she approached were strained and expressionless.

"Where's Pete?" she called. "I've come to wish him well."

The faces winced; perhaps she'd spoken more loudly than she'd thought. She lowered her voice to a theatrical whisper. "I've come to wish him well. Where is he?"

Martha Heathcote shot her a look of disgust, and Temperance felt momentarily wounded, before remembering that Martha Heathcote was a haughty bitch and always had been. She was just about to gesture something to this effect when she saw her husband striding towards her.

"I've come!" she said, presenting herself delightedly. "I've come after all to celebrate."

He grabbed her by the arm—a little violently, she thought—and pulled her back onto the grass. "What in God's name has got into you?"

"Nothing," she said and put her hand in front of her mouth to conceal a belch. "Excuse me."

"Temperance!" John said, dropping her arm. His mouth had fallen open. "You're drunk."

"No," she said, folding her arms nonchalantly—or at least, she felt, in a way that suggested nonchalance. She'd forgotten what it looked like. "Not a bit. Dry as a bone."

"Temperance." He stepped towards her, his voice softening. "Sarah. What happened to you?"

"Oh, don't go making a fuss, John. I had a small drink, same as you do every day of your life." She uncrossed her arms. "What's become of Pete Darling? I'm here to congratulate him."

He brought his hand up to her arm—gently this time. "Pete's dead, Temp."

She swung around and faced him, rocking. "What?"

"Pete Darling's dead. Murdered."

"Murdered?" She struggled to find her way around the word. "By whom?"

"That lad Mildmay. The Mansfields' farmhand."

"Thomas?"

"That's him."

She blinked. "Thomas Mildmay murdered Pete Darling on his wedding day?"

"Yes."

He pressed her into his chest, where she didn't at that moment want to be. She struggled free. "Why would he do that? What grudge did he have against Pete?"

"He's in love with Anne Mansfield, that's what he said."

Of course, she thought, Thomas Mildmay is in love with Anne Mansfield. She had seen it in his face that day at the Swan; he had longed to leave Little Nettlebed, but something had tethered him there.

John didn't meet her eye. "Pete was pursuing the Mansfield sisters because he thought they'd set out to ruin his wedding."

"Ruin—? How?"

"Barking. There was barking outside the church. Pete was convinced it was the girls, come to taunt him."

She stared at him. "Was it the girls? Did anyone see them?"

"We don't know," he said. "We didn't see. But they were there, with Mildmay and the Wildgoose brothers, when we found Pete's body."

"Oh," she said, balling her fists and pacing unsteadily. "What a *fool*. I knew he was—of course I did. All his crazy talk about the Mansfield girls . . . I tried to stop him, I really did."

"Now, Temperance, stop it. It wasn't your fault. It was unfortunate. A tragedy."

She kept pacing. "I knew it was trouble the moment I first heard Pete talk about what he'd seen across the river. Someone was bound to get hurt."

John gestured for her to lower her voice, but she didn't. This was death they were discussing. Murder. It wasn't a piece of gossip to be whispered at the alehouse. She spoke louder.

"Where is he? The boy?"

John looked at the ground. "We took him. We locked him up at Humphrey Bullock's house until the justice of the peace has been to visit."

Temperance turned to him, aghast. "What will happen to him?"

The ruddiness fell from John's face: his skin was like bone. "I don't know, Temp. He confessed to murder—"

"He'll hang," she said.

"Yes," he said softly.

She lifted her gaze to the church. "Where's Pete? Where's his body?"

"Some of the men went to fetch it. They'll be along soon."

She saw them approaching across the river, four men with Pete's body on their shoulders. They'd draped his jacket over his head and chest, but his long legs—feet knocking against each other, smart wedding shoes scuffed—stuck out uncovered. They made their way across the rock, treading gingerly. At one point, one of them stumbled, and Temperance saw the flash of Pete's dangling arm, his large hand gesturing to the riverbed. They walked through the grass towards the road, and people averted their eyes as they drew nearer, turning their heads into one another's shoulders. The crowd had been muttering before, but now an unearthly silence descended.

Temperance watched them until they disappeared up the

lane to Pete's cottage. She spun towards John. "I'm going to see him."

He raised his eyebrows. "He's dead, Temp. They just carried him past."

"Not Pete. Pete's dead." She frowned, focussing. "Thomas—I'm going to see Thomas."

John shook his head, his eyes wide. "What would possess you to do that?"

"I want to hear what he's got to say."

"I told you. He killed Pete to protect Anne Mansfield."

She made a *pah* sound with her mouth. "That lad isn't the murdering sort," she said, marching up the road towards the Bullocks' house.

John didn't follow; perhaps he was embarrassed. She didn't care. No—in fact, it was better this way. Men were like clams, lips sealing in each other's presence. It was best if she saw him alone.

She was wheezing by the time she reached the Bullocks' house. Raised voices within obscured her knocking, so she knocked harder. At last, a vexed-looking maid answered, and Temperance asked to be taken through to see the boy. Samuel Tubb and Humphrey Bullock were standing at the door to the parlour, their arms crossed. "I'm here to talk to Thomas," she announced.

They blinked. "We're not allowing visitors," Bullock said.

"I need to talk to him," Temperance said.

They looked indignant. Bullock's eyebrows knitted together. Tubb's lips became thin.

"The man is a criminal, a murderer," Bullock said, his arms folded so tightly they almost touched his chin. "No one can talk to him until the justice of the peace has arrived."

Despite all the Sunday mornings she'd spent in church since childhood, Temperance wasn't particularly religious. God was like the vicar: she knew everything about him, but he had never shown any interest in her. He hadn't been there when her father died or when her mother followed, a few years later. She hadn't felt him on her wedding day, or in those early bewildering weeks working at the Swan. He wasn't with her, each passing month, when no pregnancy appeared; she had weathered that alone. She accepted this calmly and didn't begrudge him his absence. There were more important people, kings and queens and princes, who required his attention. That day, though, standing in the dim passage, she could have sworn she felt something. A presence encompassed her, a warmth. She believed herself capable of anything, whatever she set her mind to, for God was smiling on her. She concentrated very hard. The men looked at her oddly.

Just then, a wail sounded from the back of the house. Temperance stood as if in a trance while people moved around her. "Agnes," Bullock muttered and marched away.

She turned back to the parlour. Tubb faced her, chin raised. "Oh, come off it, Tubb," she said. "Let me see him, just for a moment."

"I will not," he said, fixing his eyes above her head.

"If you do, you can drink freely at the Swan until Pete Darling is buried."

He eyed her, untrusting. "No cost at all?"

"None—if you let me see the boy."

His thin lips stretched into a grin. "Quick, then," he said. "Before Bullock gets back."

The parlour was dark. She found the glow of Thomas's luminous curls in the corner. He was hunched, his chin resting forlornly on his chest. She staggered towards him. "There you are, lad," she said.

"Mistress Shirly," he said, half standing. "What are you doing here?"

"I've come to see you," she said simply, and took a seat across from him.

He lowered himself down. His hands were tied behind his back with ribbon. She could see he'd been crying.

"What happened?" she asked.

A groan rose from deep in Thomas's throat. "Pete Darling—he was threatening the girls. They were in danger."

"So you killed him?"

"I—" He fell silent, head bowed once more.

"To protect Anne Mansfield?"

He looked up then, his face animated. "I love her," he said.

She nodded. Yes: she could see this was true.

He shifted in his chair. "I—" he said again.

His lips met and parted soundlessly, and he cleared his throat. Temperance sensed a secret demanding to be told. She'd seen it before, drunks at the alehouse trying to give voice to their troubles. Usually, all it took was time and ale. After a few hours, a few pints, they were ready to unburden everything. But she had no ale to offer Thomas, nor time. She looked at him squarely. "Whatever it is," she said, "you'd better hurry up and say it. There won't be another opportunity, and Bullock will be back soon."

"Please, Mistress Shirly," he said, his eyes shining. "You have to help me escape. I'm innocent. I didn't do it."

"But you told them you did?"

He nodded. She felt suddenly sobered, her mind quick.

"To protect someone? Anne Mansfield?"

He cleared his throat. "Not Anne."

"Someone in the village?"

She thought back to what John had said, about finding the girls with the body. About the Wildgoose brothers being there.

"No," she said. A coldness crept around her heart. "Robin?"

He looked at her; she saw it in his eyes. "No," she said again.

"Pete was threatening the girls," he said quietly. "He nearly strangled me to death."

"Not Robin," she said, shaking her head. "He's such a gentle boy."

Thomas shuffled forward. "Please. You have to help me."

She faced him, unseeing, then exhaled and focussed, fumbling in the pocket of her apron. "It's funny," she said. "I've never known the river like this, not in all my years of living here. So weak, it is now—you can barely see it. The rest of the riverbed is like a battleground, all strewn with carcasses and husks." She drew the keen-edged shell out of her pocket. "I picked this up on my way over. I don't know why. It's sharp—I wanted to make sure nobody stepped on it. It would go right through a flimsy shoe."

She looked at it for a long moment, admiring the opalescent interior, the slicing lip.

"You know," she continued. "I've had a bit to drink today. The first drink I've ever had. It does curious things to the body, I've noticed. Makes one clumsy. Butterfingered."

The shell clattered to the floor. For a moment, she allowed her eyes to rest on it, then she flashed a glance at the window. Thomas followed her eyes from the shell to the window.

"Godspeed," she said in a low voice, rising from her seat. "You did a brave thing, protecting that boy."

Tubb gave her a wink as she came out of the parlour. She no

longer felt unsteady; now she felt only sick. Outside, she dawdled for a while, drawing in deep lungfuls of fresh air, before walking towards the gate. She cast a last look at the house, at the window, its many diamond panes glittering in the sun. That poor boy, she thought. She hoped he would live.

TWENTY-FIVE

The house was quiet when Joseph Mansfield returned. "Girls?" he called, clutching the lintel of the door, but they didn't reply. He assured himself that they were up in their rooms, that they couldn't hear him, and—trusting that they had a little time before they must leave the village—he wearily sought a moment's rest. Sitting in the parlour, he heard them come in. "Girls?" he called again, and their dresses rustled as they gathered at the door.

"Yes, Grandfather?" he heard Anne say—or someone he thought must be Anne. Her voice was changed in some way.

"Where have you been?" he said.

He tried to sound angry but found that the words leaving his mouth sounded merely old-mannish. He was tired.

"We've been in the garden," said Anne, or Anne's strange twin.

"I've just walked through the garden," Joseph said. "I didn't notice you there."

Someone else spoke—Hester, he thought, but again her voice was different somehow.

"You didn't see us, Grandfather," she said. "You walked right by us."

The girls were lying to him. He hadn't known them to do that before.

"There was a disturbance up at the church," he said. "In the middle of the service, people shouting outside."

He paused, but the girls didn't speak.

"Hopefully it won't have unsettled them for long," he continued. "They will have turned their attention to drinking by now."

He paused again, and this time he heard the whisper of their clothes as they glanced at one another. He heard something else: Mary crying quietly. He reached forward and found her face, which was wet with tears.

"My child!" he said. "What's wrong?"

"Nothing," she mumbled and turned her face away from him, burying it in somebody's skirt.

"We're all tired," he said. "We've been working too hard since Connie and Amie left. Go upstairs—get some rest. Tomorrow we're taking a long trip."

He heard hushed gasps and fingers toying restlessly with stray curls. "What do you mean, Grandfather?" Elizabeth said. "Why are we leaving?"

"After the commotion at the church, I don't think it's safe for us to stay here. People are very angry with us, it seems."

Grace spoke, a child-sound, a bleat: "But where will we go?"

He tried to appear calm. "It's hard to say. I hope we can stay with friends, someone to give us a loan while things settle here. I might need to find some work."

"You've lived here your whole life, Grandfather," Anne said. "This beautiful house—you can't leave it."

He turned towards her voice, still not quite believing it. "We have to leave. The villagers have an appetite for violence."

He steadied himself with a hand on the table. The girls felt very far from him. "Go," he said. "Pack some light things. Don't leave the house, any of you."

He heard them shuffle away. "Wait," he said. "Where's Mildmay? I told him to stay with you."

More rustlings, this time louder. "Well?"

He could hear Mary draw a stilted breath. "He's going back to the moon," she said. "That's where he's from, you know. The moon."

Joseph, mystified, heard the others look down at their sister. "Why do you say that, Mary?" Elizabeth asked.

Fabric lifted, the sound of shrugging shoulders. "Robin Wildgoose said so, I heard him. He said Thomas's days on earth are numbered." She paused. "He sounded very sorrowful, so I knew it was true."

They hesitated. "This is nonsense," Anne said at last. "Mary's making up stories. Mildmay isn't here because I sent him out . . . to the market."

Her voice was now so changed that Joseph found himself stepping forward, blinking at her shadowy face.

"Why did you do that? I asked for him to be here with you."

She paused. "I needed rose water for your eyes. All our roses are finished."

Joseph drew a quick breath. She was using his own sightlessness to lie to him. The boy wasn't out buying rose water—that much Joseph knew—but where he was he couldn't fathom. At that moment, he didn't care. He felt betrayed by the girls. He wanted respite from their lies.

"Go," he said. "Now. Upstairs. Gather your things. Get some rest."

They left, and he allowed quietness to reign. Occasionally, he heard creakings from the floorboards above, but no voices carried down to him. He lowered himself into a chair and sat there, motionless, for a long time, summoning the strength for the journey ahead.

* * *

HE MUST HAVE dozed; the room seemed darker, and there was an ache in his neck. He pushed himself to his feet and found his way to the hall. "Anne?" he called, but heard nothing.

He walked slowly up the stairs, his skin ringing. He couldn't seem to take in enough air. What did he fear he might find? She was a good girl; she had never deceived him. But that was the old Anne, a voice within him said. The new, changed Anne is perfectly capable of deceiving you.

"Anne?" he shouted again.

Hearing movement in one of the bedrooms, he pushed open the door. "Where is she?"

"She's in her room, Grandfather," Hester said.

"Why doesn't she answer me, then?" He turned away.

"Wait," Grace said.

"What is it?"

"Leave her for a moment, please, Grandfather. She needs to be alone."

"What's the matter with her?"

"Nothing—"

"But she needs to be alone?"

"She's sad to leave tomorrow. We all are."

Joseph made a low sound. "I'll talk to her."

He heard whispering as he crossed the corridor.

"Anne?" he said, knocking loudly.

The door opened, and he found Anne standing there. He could dimly see something awful in her face. "Anne," he said again, softer this time. "What's wrong?"

He struggled to make sense of what was happening. He couldn't explain it; something was being concealed from him, but he didn't know what. Anne was behaving so strangely—this girl he knew so well. He felt wary of her, as though she were a wild creature which required careful handling.

"Nothing, Grandfather," she said. "I wish to be alone."

She had never dismissed him before. He took a step back.

"Are you angry with me, child?"

"No," she said, but he heard it in her voice. "I just want to be alone."

There was shouting outside, by the gate. Even in the gloomy corridor, Joseph could see Anne whiten. "Someone's here," he said. "I'll go and send them away. Stay inside, do you hear me?"

He fumbled downstairs and found his way to the door. He must have slept for some time, lulled by the belief that the villagers would be distracted by the revelries, and that he and the girls could safely make their departure in the morning. But what if he'd left it too late? Dusk had now descended, mystifying his eyes. He peered into the gloaming. There: he could make out a figure at the bottom of the garden, illuminated by the last bruises of pink light on the horizon. Something ghostly dropped from one of the apple trees—Catchrat, come to greet him. He pressed past her, his mouth dry.

"Good evening," he called as he approached the gate. "Who's there?"

"It's Bullock," a voice said from the shadows.

"Ah. Enjoying the festivities, I trust? I'm sorry I couldn't join you after the ceremony."

He heard spluttering. "Haven't you heard, Mansfield?" Bullock said.

"Heard what?" Joseph said. He couldn't make out Bullock's face at all.

"Pete Darling was murdered shortly after the wedding," Bullock said, sounding choked. "He was stabbed by Thomas Mildmay. We've been holding Mildmay until the justice of the peace arrives, but he managed to escape. I believe he's here."

Joseph staggered, as though he'd been pushed. "No," he said under his breath.

"Please let me in so I can find the boy."

"Are you alone?"

"Yes. That wretch Samuel Tubb took off for the alehouse."

"Well, come, if you must. But I should warn you, you won't find the boy here. I haven't seen him since this morning."

The men said nothing to each other as they walked up to the house. Joseph didn't trust his own voice. "Here," he said. "The boy's lodgings are over there. You may search them if you like."

Bullock crossed the yard. From Thomas's room he went to the stables and from there he returned to the house. Joseph stood at the door, waiting.

"Excuse me, sir," Bullock said, breathless. "I'll need to search the building."

"Now, Bullock, I've been sitting in my parlour all afternoon. The boy has not come in here."

Bullock's voice grew very high and strained. "You are virtually blind, sir. You won't have seen the lad come in. If you don't mind—my daughter is weeping at home, widowed on her wedding day. I must help her somehow. I must find the man who did this."

He stepped towards Mansfield, his breath hot and scented with ale. Joseph heard movement behind him.

"It's all right, Grandfather," Anne said. She was carrying two candles which bathed her face in yellow light. "Let Mister Bullock come and look for Thomas. We hope it will bring Miss Agnes peace of mind."

Joseph shook his head and stepped to one side. He was so weary. He didn't look at Anne, but, standing beside her, he felt her whole body trembling. She passed one of the candles to Bullock, and they listened as he went into the parlour, the hall, the larder, the kitchen. They listened and said nothing, their breath shallow.

"How about upstairs?" Bullock said, but Joseph could hear that some of the fire in his voice had been extinguished.

"The boy is not upstairs. Those are our bedrooms, my granddaughters' and mine—"

A shrill creak cut through his words, carrying from the floorboards above.

"My sisters are up there," Anne said. "They're very distressed after the day's events."

A pause. "Mildmay said that he was defending you from Pete Darling," Bullock said. "That Darling was half-crazed, that he wanted to hurt you."

Anne exhaled; her candle flickered briskly. "You must have heard him, sir," she said. "He was intent on ruining us."

"My son-in-law had some very regrettable notions," Bullock said. "I'd warned him against these ideas myself, but he refused to listen . . . He wasn't worthy of my daughter, you know."

Joseph groped for a suitable response but could think of

nothing. He drew a breath of greasy, tallow-scented air to soothe himself. He was aware that his role as Mildmay's master made him indebted to the Bullocks in some way. "Can we offer you anything, sir? Some food, perhaps?"

"No," Bullock said, stepping out into the yard. "I must be going. I'll be back soon. The justice of the peace will want to speak with you, I'm sure."

"Of course," Joseph said. "Good evening, sir." He closed the door and stood in the passage with his eyes closed.

"Grandfather?"

"Is he here?"

"I—"

Joseph growled. "He can't stay."

"He isn't—"

"He must leave. Tonight."

She breathed in sharply.

"You're deceiving me, Anne."

She shook her head.

He paused. "Did he do it—did he kill Pete Darling?"

"No," she said. Something in her tone made him feel afraid. It seemed more essential than ever that they should leave first thing.

"Bring some food up to my room, will you? I'm very tired."

"Of course." She was close; he could feel the warmth of the candle on his face. "Thank you, Grandfather. I know this has been hard."

"Yes," he said, passing his hand over his opened mouth, his chin. "But you know I would do anything—" He stopped. "You are very dear to me, all of you."

He turned his face away from her.

"Should anyone need them, there are some coins in my study. I won't miss them."

Something heavy had been poured into his body, weighing down his limbs like lead. He ate the food that Anne brought up to him and allowed her to kiss him on the cheek when she took away his bowl. He fell quickly into sleep.

He slept deeply, dreaming of his wife and son. He saw clearly in his dreams; that night the colours were brighter than ever, their faces vivid. He found the threads of silver in his wife's hair, the mirthful creases around her mouth and eyes. Before him was his son's face—the familiar gap between his teeth and the thin white scar above one eyebrow. Soon, the scene changed; his wife and son faded, replaced by his bedroom, bathed in blue moonlight. He saw the embroidered flowers in the tapestry hanging around his bed, scarlet petals bursting into bud. He saw his hands, his body beneath the coverlets. It occurred to him, rising unsteadily to his feet, that he must still be dreaming. Even in the bright moonlight, he would never normally see so well.

All the richness of the night was concentrated into his sight. He heard nothing—not a whisper or a sigh. Sometimes he could hear Mary muttering in her sleep, or Hester and Grace talking softly, but tonight there was no sound at all. Perhaps he would check on them. He was sorry not to have eaten with them yesterday evening; he didn't want them to think him angry. Yes, he would see how they were. Take in their moonlit faces. Find them in their childhood rooms for a final time before they left the next day.

He went to the youngest girls' room first, amazed at how much he could see. He didn't need his hands to guide him;

the way was clear. At the door he hesitated, bewildered by his racing heartbeat. There was no danger here, he told himself. The girls were sleeping soundly. But when he pushed open the door, he saw that he was mistaken, that his racing heart was right: the beds were empty. The girls were not there.

His feet carried him across to the other room—also empty. Everything arranged neatly, eerily unstirring. The house was silent as a crypt, and he was alone.

A sound cut through the quietness. Something moving, rustling, in the garden. Branches cracking, feet padding through tall grass. Joseph crept to the window and saw the orchard through uneven panes. Everything was silver and still, ripening apples awash with white light. He saw Catchrat, clear as crystal, darting through the dark undergrowth—away from what?

Joseph's heart stopped when he saw them. There were dogs in the orchard, five of them. Panting and tall, pink tongues hanging from fanged mouths. A boy crouched among them, hair glinting in the glow of the moon. They circled each other and then, without warning, they began to run. Five dogs and a boy, moving through the orchard, leaping the wall, leaving him.

Joseph fumbled with the window, pushing it wide. "No," he shouted as loudly as his lungs would allow. "Come back!"

But they didn't hear him, or perhaps they no longer knew the words.

His hand still on the window, he began to sob. His granddaughters. Those beloved girls—gone. Why had they left him? Where would they go? He squinted into the wooded land beyond the wall but saw nothing. The dogs, the girls, had disappeared completely.

His shoulders slumped. He had seen them. Beautiful dogs, fierce and full of power. Amid his grief and his fear, he found another feeling—gladness. The old thought returned to him, that he'd rather they were dogs than damaged girls. He'd rather they were free than confined by him.

Something moved across the sky, something foreign and plump: a cloud. Joseph smelled moisture, the rich scent of coming rain. It was too much—the unfathomable sights, the smells. He felt dazzled by it all; he longed for darkness once more.

Taking a last look at the garden, he stumbled back to bed and pulled his coverlets over himself. There he slept, or continued to sleep, until morning, when Humphrey Bullock returned with a mob and the justice of the peace. The sound of angry men pierced through a pleasant dream Joseph was having, a dream about sisters and dogs and the longed-for end to a season of feverish drought.

ACKNOWLEDGEMENTS

To my agent Holly Faulks I give heartfelt thanks—I am deeply grateful for your enduring belief in my work. Thank you to all at Greene & Heaton, particularly Kate Rizzo and Mia Dakin. At Triangle House Literary, I am indebted to Emma Dries.

Working with such thoughtful, keen-eyed editors has been an enormous privilege. Thank you so much to Caroline Zancan, Amy Batley, and Charlotte Cray for taking on this book and making it better.

Thank you to the wonderful teams at Hutchinson Heinemann and Henry Holt. At Hutchinson Heinemann, I am especially grateful to Rose Waddilove, Sarah Bance, Mary Chamberlain, Ceara Elliot, Isabella Levin, and Isabelle Ralphs. At Holt, I owe huge thanks to Leela Gebo, Chris O'Connell, Molly Lindley Pisani, Sarah Bowen, Nicolette Seeback Ruggiero, Laura Flavin, Sonja Flancher, Abigail Novak, and Sam Wiener.

For their illuminating work on this historical period, I would like to acknowledge Bernard Capp, Patricia Crawford, Tara Hamling, Sara Heller Mendelson, Ralph Houlbrooke, Ian Mortimer, Peter Razzell, Catherine Teresa Richardson, Ruth Scurr, and Keith Thomas. Robert Gibbings's deep knowledge of the flora and fauna of the River Thames has also taught me much.

I am fortunate to have been cheered on in my writing journey by many enthusiastic friends and wider family members—I am thankful for them all. For special encouragement and advice, I would like to thank Katherine Bucknell, Claudia Costa-Rowse, Poppy Franks, Michael Guppy, Olivia Henry, Charlotte Neil, Sara-Ella Ozbek, Otegha Uwagba, and Polly West. I am profoundly grateful for the support of my beloved family: my siblings, Kerensa, Lucian, and Eila, and my parents, Phillida and Christopher, to whom this book is dedicated. Finally, for the daily gifts they give me—the enriching love and enlivening joy—I thank my husband, Will, and our son, Clement.

ABOUT THE AUTHOR

Xenobe Purvis was born in Tokyo in 1990. She studied English literature at the University of Oxford, has an MA in creative writing from Royal Holloway, and was part of the London Library's Emerging Writers Programme. She is a writer and literary researcher, with essays published in the *Times Literary Supplement*, the *London Magazine*, and elsewhere.